FOR PAUL &
FELLOW B-
AND FRIEND.
HOPE the book brings
back some MEMORIES.
Warm REGARDS,

NOBLE CAUSE

A suspense novel set in the Cold War
about the B-47 bomber
and the men who flew her

John McCartan
Colonel, USAF (Ret.)
Aug. 2008

Robert O. McCartan

Noble Cause

A suspense novel set in the Cold War about the B-47 bomber and the men who flew her

Published by Wheatmark™
610 East Delano Street, Suite 104
Tucson, Arizona 85705 U.S.A.
www.wheatmark.com

International Standard Book Number: 978-1-58736-921-6
Library of Congress Control Number: 2007933242

Cover photo courtesy of 307th Bomb Wing Association.

I want to thank the following for their help, their support, and their encouragement in writing this novel. Without them it could not have been done: Connie Paul Kazal; Maurine Kish; Meg Park; Sue Kaib McCartan; and Bill MacLaren. And, of course, I want to thank my children: Mike, Carrie, and Andy for their constant support.

Thank you all.

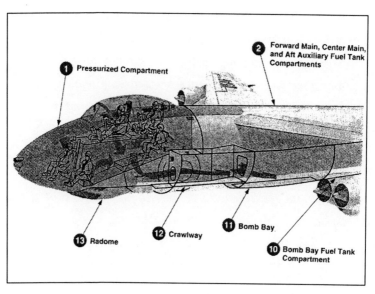

The B-47 bomber crew movement and compartments.

This book is dedicated to the thousands of men who flew the B-47 jet bomber during the Cold War. Part of the Strategic Air Command, these men toiled long hours, day after day, in freezing skies and dark mole holes around the world, waiting for the klaxon to sound in the middle of the night—a signal that would send them to nuclear war against the Soviets. These committed fliers sacrificed family and higher-paying civilian jobs for the honor and privilege to serve their country in its time of need. Their professionalism and dedication helped keep America free from attack during the 1950s and early 1960s. I am proud to have been one of them.

Chapter 1

As an early morning thunderstorm ended, Lieutenant Troy Bench opened the canopy on his T-38 jet trainer while taxiing back to his squadron operations. The high-pitched whine of the two J-85 engines and the pungent exhaust from their tail pipes blended with the sweet dampness of the cotton fields surrounding Williams Air Force Base near Phoenix. Troy felt a surge of exhilaration. He was about to fly his first jet solo mission.

"Okay, Lieutenant," came the instructor's voice from the rear cockpit. "Go fly this bird just like you've been doing for the last two weeks, and don't skip any checklist items." With an encouraging slap on Troy's shoulder, the instructor climbed down and disappeared into the operations building.

"Tiger Zero-four, you're cleared to taxi, runway three-zero, right," came a transmission from the control tower.

Nudging the throttles forward with the palm of his left hand, Troy felt the surge of the two powerful J-85s vibrating through the airframe. This was the moment he had been waiting for. Although sensing some anxiety, he felt comfortable in the cockpit of the swept-winged jet. He had worked hard and was determined to be the top pilot in his class.

As he taxied, Troy's mind raced through the myriad of procedures he needed to complete after takeoff. This time no instructor would remind him if he missed a checklist item. He was on his own.

"Williams Tower, Tiger Zero-four, ready for takeoff."

"Zero-four, you're cleared for immediate takeoff. Climb to and maintain fifteen thousand feet, turn heading two-four-zero after takeoff. Good day, sir."

Troy closed the clamshell canopy, lined up on the runway, and eased the throttles forward. Releasing the brakes, he stayed on the centerline as the jet sped down the runway. He felt pressure against his back from the thrust as the two engines clawed their way toward becoming airborne. At the 2,500-foot marker, the aircraft lifted into the air. Troy retracted the gear and flaps and set the throttles for a three-hundred-knot climb-out. Glancing downward, he saw the shadowy reflection of his aircraft race across the geometric patchwork of green cotton fields quickly growing smaller beneath him.

Switching the radios to Phoenix Center frequency, he reached down with his gloved hand and adjusted the air-conditioning vents. The blast of icy air felt invigorating against the nervous perspiration that drenched his flight suit. Knowing he was in sole command of his jet, Troy felt confident as he guided the aircraft through a broken layer of cumulus clouds. He had wanted to be a pilot since his first flight in an open-cockpit Stearman at the age of twelve.

Scanning the engine instruments, he made a mental note of the slightly higher-than-normal exhaust gas temperature on the left engine. He momentarily forgot to level off as he passed through fifteen thousand feet, but he corrected by pushing the nose over to maintain his assigned altitude.

"Phoenix Center, Tiger Zero-four, request permission to continue climbing to twenty-four thousand and proceed to Williams Practice Area Number 2."

"Zero-four, you're cleared to Williams Number 2. Maintain twenty-four thousand feet."

Troy eased the throttles forward to initiate the climb. Suddenly, a violent explosion in the rear engine bay jerked his body forward with such force that his helmet slammed against the canopy. The engine instruments plummeted toward zero, and both engine EGTs pegged into the red. The stench of molten metal crept into the cockpit as the airplane rolled left and pitched up. Troy pushed the nose over to keep from stalling and wrenched the wings back to level flight. The aircraft began to shudder.

"*Mayday! Mayday!* Tiger Zero-four, engine failure!" he shouted over his emergency UHF channel.

Acrid smoke seeped into the cockpit, stinging his eyes. He gasped for air. Tightening his mask and chin strap, he switched to 100-percent pressure oxygen and mentally ran through the ejection sequence. As the flight instruments became murky, he realized the engines were destroying themselves. Attempting an engine restart would have been futile—he had to get out.

"Tiger Zero-four, this is Phoenix Center. Can we be of assistance?"

"Roger, Phoenix. Vector me away from populated areas. I've gotta get out of this thing."

"Turn to heading two-two-zero. We've alerted Williams Field of your emergency. Rescue equipment is being launched. We're tracking you."

Troy was surprised by how calm he was. Everything became sequential and mechanical; the Air Force had trained him well. Turning to the new heading, he glanced at the altimeter through watery, burning eyes. He could barely make out the stubby needle as it passed through eight thousand feet. The controls became mushy and unresponsive. It was time to eject.

He yanked the clear plastic visor down over his

eyes until it locked in place. Tucking his legs in tightly, he gripped the yellow-striped handles on both sides of the ejection seat, squeezed the triggers with all of his strength, and pulled up hard.

It was as if a mule had kicked him in the ass. The canopy exploded away from the airplane, and he was hurtled from one hostile environment into another. A two-hundred-mile-per-hour blast of air snapped his head back as he catapulted through space, arms flailing. Within seconds, the explosive bolts in the ejection mechanism separated him from the seat.

Immediately Troy's body stabilized. He could hear only the gentle fluttering of the red-and-white canopy of nylon above him. His mind raced back to the five practice jumps he had made at the Air Force Academy the year before. What could he remember about parachute landings?

Looking down from about two thousand feet, he saw a bright fireball followed by a huge mushroom cloud of black smoke; his million-dollar airplane had just burrowed itself into the ground. Simultaneously, the inhospitable Arizona desert, strewn with jagged rocks and cacti, rushed up toward him. He landed hard and rolled.

Before Troy could retrieve the emergency radio from his survival seat-pack, he heard the sound of a rescue helicopter. As he stood up, his limbs seemed to be in working order, but he was puzzled by an intense burning sensation over his right side and back. Upon closer examination, he realized the source of the pain: he had landed in a giant cluster of desert cholla and prickly-pear cacti.

....

Mark Denman, Troy's roommate at the Air Force Academy and also his best friend, was the first visitor at the base hospital. As Mark entered the room, two nurses were tucking in Troy's bed sheets and adjusting the drip tube into his left forearm. They cautioned Lieutenant Denman to stay for only a few minutes.

"Good Lord, man, you're one lucky son of a bitch," Mark said as Troy squirmed from side to side in the hospital bed. "How are you feeling?"

"Fine, except for my backside. Stings like hell, and I can't find a comfortable position."

"You just *had* to land in the only damn brier patch within miles," Mark said, with a grin. "Anyway, congratulations on getting out of the thing alive. That was some good heads-up flying, Troy!"

"What's the word around the squadron?" Troy asked. "Bet the commander's pissed about losing an airplane."

"All I've heard were good things. Down in the squadron, we didn't know what had happened to you at first, so we were pretty worried. There were lots of wild rumors flying around. Once we found out what had happened, everyone—including the command-er—was talking about what a shit-hot job you did."

Mark moved closer to the bed and lit a cigarette. "In fact, he mentioned something about you conducting a briefing for the wing when you felt better. You know—what you did right, what you'd do differently, that kind of thing."

Mark looked around the room for an ashtray. "I heard the commander say that you'd be grounded for just a few days until the accident investigation board completes their work."

"God, I hope you're right, Mark, and they don't drag this thing out. I'm anxious to get back to flying."

"By the way, Troy, I called Wendy to let her know you were okay. Didn't want your wife to hear about you on the twelve o'clock Phoenix news. She's on her way out. Hey, gotta run. I have a flight in an hour, but I'll try and stop by later this evening."

"Thanks, Mark, and thanks for checking on me."

Chapter II

THE ACCIDENT INVESTIGATION BOARD took only a week to determine that the left J-85 engine of Troy's jet had lost several turbine blades, causing it to explode and drive debris into the right engine, ultimately resulting in catastrophic power failure. Troy was commended for his quick thinking and accurate response to the in-flight emergency and for steering his craft away from population areas.

....

During the next nine months of training, Troy achieved his goal of graduating at the top of his pilot training class, but he was disappointed to find that there were no fighter assignments available at the time—only bomber quotas. Yet Troy quickly recovered and vowed to do his best in his assignment with the Strategic Air Command, or SAC, flying their new swept-wing, six-engine B-47 jet bomber at March Air Force Base in Southern California.

Before reporting to March, Troy had two weeks' leave. He and Wendy had been married for more than a year, and because of his tight flying schedule, they had not been able to spend much time with Troy's parents. So, they decided to take the opportunity to visit them in Troy's hometown of Bisbee, Arizona.

On their way out of Phoenix, Troy and Wendy stopped at the GM dealership to trade in Troy's twelve-year-old Ford as down payment on a hot new fire-engine red Corvette with white leather seats. After all, he now had a real job with a real paycheck at the end of every month.

Pointing their new sports car south, they drove down Highway 80 toward Bisbee with the top down and Wendy's shoulder-length blonde hair blowing freely in the breeze — every bit the scene out of a James Dean movie.

The son of immigrant parents, Troy was a first-generation American who had grown up in the small mining town of Bisbee. His mother was born and raised in Sonora, Mexico, and his father had emigrated from a small mountain village in Czechoslovakia. Upon arriving in the United States, Troy's father had Americanized his name by shortening it from "Stepffen Benchovic" to "Steven Bench." His mother had followed suit by changing "Angelica Antoinette" to "Angie."

Troy's dad had recently retired from the Phelps Dodge Copper Company and his parents had moved into a more comfortable home in the small Bisbee suburb of Warren.

Approaching the picturesque mountain town of Bisbee, Wendy's mind lapsed back to memories of previous visits with Troy's parents. She enjoyed being around them and looked forward to another visit. With such diverse backgrounds, she had been curious about how they had met.

"Troy, with your parents' cultural differences, how in the world did they ever get together?"

"As I recall, they met at a dance competition one Saturday night at the CIO Miners Union Hall. My parents laugh about it now, but my dad insists it was his handsome looks and his Charles Atlas body that attracted my mom. Of course, Mom denies all of that." Troy glanced over at Wendy with a grin. "I have no doubt that there was a huge physical attraction between them, though. And it's still there! My father never misses an opportunity to pat my mom on her behind. Also, I think they had a lot of other things in common. They were both hard workers, and they were committed to making the American dream happen for them. Of course, it didn't hurt that they were both devout Catholics and wanted a family."

Troy had been away from Bisbee much of the past five years—four years at the Air Force Academy and almost a year in pilot training. The week in Bisbee went by all too soon. It was comfortable for Troy to be home again around old friends and family.

Packing the Corvette with their luggage and the food that Troy's mom had prepared for them, Troy and Wendy said their good-byes and pointed the sports car northward for a week of rafting on the Colorado River.

Troy's leave soon came to an end. Wendy still had a year to finish work on her degree at Arizona State University, and although Troy and Wendy would be separated for a time, they felt it was important that Wendy complete her schooling. They decided to keep the apartment in Tempe. Wendy's good friend Annabelle DeLuca moved in with her.

Troy was excited to be headed for his first Air Force operational assignment. The anticipation of what was in store for him at March AFB was overwhelming. Including his time at the Academy, he had waited a long five years for this assignment.

Leaving Wendy at their Tempe apartment after some long good-byes, Troy pointed his Corvette west toward California. As the monotony of the mesquite-ridden Arizona desert unfolded before him, his mind drifted to thoughts of Wendy and memories of the past two weeks.

He smiled, remembering the morning their small raft flipped over in the whitewater rapids of the ice-cold Colorado River. After dragging themselves onto the bank, bruised and shivering, they had held each other tightly and laughed as they watched their brand-new backpacks bobbing down the river, most certainly destined for the Gulf of California. He reflected on the evening two years ago when he had asked Wendy to marry him. The lifelong promises they had whispered to each other that evening echoed in his mind. Mentally re-creating the first time they had made love, he almost drove off the road. His mood grew more serious as he recalled the tearful good-byes of a few short hours earlier when he had dropped Wendy off at the university.

Suddenly a sign, MARCH AFB NEXT RIGHT, jolted him back to reality. March was only a few miles from the nineteenth-century Spanish town of Riverside, just west of the San Jacinto Pass in Southern California. Spanish Captain Juan Bautista de Anza had discovered the fertile Riverside Valley with its lakes and sub-desert areas, which would eventually become home to some of the richest citrus groves in the world.

A sign at the base read, "Welcome to the Oldest Military Flying Installation on the West Coast." It was here during World War II that bombardment crews received their final training before departing for the South Pacific. The 22nd Bombardment Group with its B-29s had moved to March just after the war. The base's two-and-a-half-mile-long runway was well suited for the multiengine B-47 jets that arrived there in the mid-1950s.

The sergeant at the gate checked Troy's orders and ID and motioned him through with a crisp salute. "Welcome to the Strategic Air Command and March Air Force Base, Lieutenant."

Troy returned the salute. "Thank you, Sergeant."

March was a typical SAC base, well kept and clean. The sound of jet bombers overhead was music to his ears. Troy savored the comfortable feeling of being on a military installation; he felt like he was coming home. His first stop was at personnel, where he learned that he'd been assigned to the 64th Bomb Squadron of the 22nd Bomb Wing. On his way out of the building, he bumped into his old friend Mark Denman, who had arrived at March a week earlier.

"Troy, I can't believe our good luck," Mark said in greeting. "We're in the same squadron, and we're fortunate as hell to be in the 64th. It's the best outfit on base, with a top-notch commander—a lieutenant colonel named Jack Blauw."

Mark and Troy caught up on old times that evening at the O Club. Over several ice-cold beers, they rehashed their disappointment that no fighter assignments had been available for their pilot training class. Troy changed the subject to something more positive by relaying his and Wendy's trip to Bisbee and the week they spent rafting down the Colorado.

"So where are you living, Mark?" Troy asked after they had ordered another round.

"I'm in the bachelor officers' quarters. I think I'll just stay there for a while—it's comfortable and cheap. How about you?" Mark asked.

"Well, with Wendy in Tempe for another semester, I'll probably stay in the BOQ, too. Maybe look for an apartment for us later.

"Mark, I'm getting ready to report in tomorrow. I read Colonel Blauw's bio under his picture mounted on the wall while I was at personnel. Apparently he's a recalled reserve officer who went from lieutenant to lieutenant colonel in just five years."

"I met the man last week," Mark said. "He's the real thing: outgoing, charismatic, full of energy. And he's got the looks and charm of a Hollywood movie star. I'm told he flies a damn good airplane, too."

The following morning Troy drove to the squadron ops building. After signing in, he knocked on the partially open door of Lieutenant Colonel Blauw's office. Blauw, in a flying suit, jumped from behind the desk with his arm outstretched. Troy came to attention and saluted. "First Lieutenant Troy Bench reporting for duty, sir."

"Welcome aboard, Bench. I'm darn glad you're here. You settled in yet? Is your wife here with you?"

"Sir, I'm in the BOQ. My wife is finishing her last semester at Arizona State. I may look for an apartment later. I'm really anxious to get checked out in the airplane as soon as possible. I'll fly every day if that's what it takes."

Blauw moved toward the window to look out on a flightline loaded with row after row of swept-winged jet bombers. Turning to look at Troy, his response was slow and pensive. "You know what, Lieutenant? I'm darn short on copilots." Blauw stroked his chin thoughtfully. "Damn it, I'm gonna bend the rules and give you a local checkout. That'll put you in the air within a couple of weeks."

"Thank you, Colonel! I won't let you down."

Blauw nodded and sat down at his desk. "Most of our pilots and radar/bombardier/navigators—or bomb-navs, as we call them in this airplane—are older World War II and Korean War guys. You'll meet 'em; they're great guys and real pros. But frankly, I'm tickled to death to be getting in some young pilots and bomb-navs full of piss and vinegar. I have to tell you, Bench, there's a whole lot of top brass at SAC headquarters who still have a World War II mentality. They think the guys who fly these spanking new jets have to have a couple of wars and thousands of flying hours under their belts."

Blauw shook his head in frustration. "Those peck-erheads don't know what they're talking about. It's just another damn flying machine. You young guys are gonna do just fine."

....

Over the next couple of weeks, Troy dug in and completed ground school and the required flight sim-ulator missions in record time. It was all he could do to stay awake during the sessions on special weapons training, a deadly dull but critical subject that taught crew members the "care and feeding" of nuclear bombs.

Major Allan Kurfman, the senior aircraft com-mander and instructor pilot, or IP, in the 64th, had been hunting for a replacement copilot since his had left for a job with the airlines. After reviewing Troy's records and liking what he saw, he asked Troy to join his crew. Troy jumped at the opportunity. They met for coffee at the Club, along with Kurfman's bomb-nav, Major John Nale.

Kurfman was of medium build, a couple inches short of six feet, with a full head of wavy blond hair that seemed always to be fixed in place. He chose his words carefully and spoke slowly and deliberately with a hint of a Texas accent. He wore his uniform with pride; even his flying suits were hand pressed. Kurfman wasn't old enough for World War II, but he had flown B-29 combat missions in Korea. He and Major Nale had flown B-50s together for several years.

Nale was a rugged-looking, six-foot Texan who nearly always had a smile on his face. He had a jovial personality and the latest dirty joke ready for anyone who would listen. Nale had flown B-26s in Korea and retained a small scar over his right eye as a reminder of a crash landing at Osan following a night combat mission. As the chief bomb-nav for the squadron, he was always willing to pass on his many years of experience to anyone who needed help.

Kurfman probed Troy on his goals. When Troy related his disappointment that he hadn't gotten a fighter assignment out of pilot training, Kurfman sympathized but assured him that he would learn to love flying the B-47.

"After all, Troy," Kurfman said with a wry smile, "the B-47 is really just an overgrown fighter with a bomb bay and six jet engines. You're going to enjoy its challenges. And the biggest advantage for you is that I'm an instructor pilot and can provide you with hands-on stick time. What I want from you in return is to be the best damn copilot you can be. You'll soon find that it's not the easiest job in the world."

Troy assured Kurfman and Nale that he would throw all of his energy into learning every facet of the B-47 and crew procedures.

Chapter III

THE B-47 CAME INTO the Air Force inventory in the early 1950s as the world's first multiengine jet. It ruled the skies for more than ten years, during which it was the backbone for the Strategic Air Command's nuclear-carrying bomber fleet.

The well-trained, three-man SAC crews who flew the bomber had a love-hate relationship with her: she was a demanding, high-maintenance lady you could not ignore for even a second without risking death, but those lucky enough to fly her loved her sleek lines and speed, which were unmatched by any airplane at the time. The B-47 could climb to more than forty thousand feet in less than twenty minutes and cruise at well over five hundred miles per hour. The aircraft's advanced technological design allowed the bomber to carry all shapes and sizes of nuclear weaponry in its bomb bay.

Troy's first flight in the B-47 was scheduled for a late-evening departure. He had spent the previous day with Kurfman and Nale, flight planning the nine-hour practice combat mission. Nale had also worked with Troy the previous night, pointing out the stars and planets that he wanted Troy to "shoot" by, averaging their declination through a series of two-minute shots with the periscopic sextant.

Now, at the end of the runway, all six of the bomber's jet engines rumbled at 100 percent. The earth literally shook as Kurfman released the brakes and all 95 tons of the aircraft lumbered down the runway. Gaining speed slowly at first, the airplane began accelerating as a water-alcohol mixture was injected into the engines to augment takeoff power. Glancing over his shoulder, Troy observed huge clouds of black smoke, formed by the water-alcohol mix, swirling behind each engine. He was struck by the thunderous power of the six J-47 engines, each with 7,000 pounds of thrust. At 162 knots and more than a mile and a half down the runway, the huge bomber with its thirty-degrees swept wings lifted gracefully off the ground. On Kurfman's command, Troy retracted the landing gear and flaps. Kurfman set climb power for 320 knots, and minutes later the airplane leveled off at thirty-eight thousand feet.

Major Nale set up his computer gyros for a two-hour celestial polar navigation leg out over the Pacific. As Nale called out the approximate height and azimuth of the three stars and planets he wanted Troy to shoot, Troy averaged the readings through a two-minute period. He called back the degrees of declination to Major Nale, and after a series of computations, Nale plotted the lines of position on his chart, fixing the aircraft position by celestial means. Terminating the two-hour navigation leg, the crew shifted gears for a practice bomb run. Troy read the twelve-item bombing checklist aloud as Nale tweaked his radar to ferret out the target he was assigned to strike in the Seattle complex. Simulating the release of a nuclear weapon on the target, the bomber's release point was scored by an Air Force unit on the ground that tracked it by radar to the phantom target. The radar bomb-scoring unit transmitted the encoded circular error to the bomber crew: it was a four-hundred-footer, close enough to obliterate the target with a nuke. Troy's celestial shots turned out well, and Major Nale praised his accuracy.

Troy eagerly anticipated the needs of the aircraft commander, or A/C, and the bombardier-navigator, or bomb-nav; he was ready with their checklists when called for. The omission of even one checklist item in this airplane could easily spell disaster. He was eager to meet the expectations that Kurfman and Nale had for him.

Preparing for a night refueling, Major Nale completed an electronic rendezvous with a KC-135 tanker, directing the bomber to within one hundred meters of the tanker in orbit near the Canadian border. With its inherent dangers, airborne refueling—particularly at night and in bad weather—involved flying close formation at five hundred miles per hour. Tucked tightly under the tail of the tanker, the boom operator positioned a twenty-foot long telescoping fuel probe into a small clamshell opening on the nose of the B-47, inches from the bomb-nav's head.

Making it look easy, Kurfman carefully maneuvered the big bomber under the tail of the tanker and took on twenty thousand pounds of JP-4 fuel in just nine minutes. Troy watched every move intently while busily manipulating valves and distributing and balancing the incoming fuel loads. Not maintaining the proper center of gravity, or CG, in the B-47 could be life threatening. Kurfman disconnected and slowed to a safe distance behind the tanker.

"Okay, Troy, now I want *you* to try," Kurfman said. "Normally you'd get your first refueling in daylight, but I'm gonna let you have a go at it tonight. I think you can handle it. The main thing is to stay relaxed, don't overcorrect, and for God's sake, don't overrun the tanker."

As Troy absorbed the words he had just heard, Kurfman reached down to transmit a message.

"Boomer 30, I'd like to let my new copilot practice for a couple of minutes, okay?"

"Bronco 21, that'll be fine. Let us know if we can help."

"Okay, Troy, you've got the airplane. Now drive in slowly." Kurfman's instructions were calm and deliberate. "Remember, just small corrections."

Troy felt as if he were in the dream sequence of a movie. He couldn't believe that he was actually wrestling this ninety-ton winged behemoth in such tight quarters. He felt that he could almost reach up and touch the tanker, while the whole time both aircraft sped through the moonless night sky at five hundred miles per hour, hooked together by a four-inch aluminum telescoping pipe pumping highly volatile JP-4 at the rate of three thousand pounds a minute.

"That's it, Troy, you're doing fine," Kurfman assured him. "Now, come up slowly under the boom. Oops! Not so fast ... Okay, Troy, you've got the airplane again. This time stabilize your position first. Good, that's fine. Now move forward ... creep up slowly. That's perfect."

Kurfman chose his words of instruction carefully, articulating them slowly and calmly. "You don't need all six throttles when you're in position; just use the inboards, it'll make it much easier. That's it ... you're doing fine, just fine. No quick movements. Quick movements make the boom operator really uncomfortable.

"Troy, it helps if you pick out a reference point on the underbelly of the tanker. I like to use the horizontal stabilizer. Some pilots use the bottom of the tanker's engine nacelles. Whatever works best for ya … Okay, now relax your grip. I've got the airplane.

"Do you realize that you stayed hooked up for four whole minutes? And I gotta tell ya, that's damn good for a first try—particularly at night."

Troy's flying suit was drenched with perspiration. "I have to confess, sir, that's the most challenging and physically exhausting thing I've ever done in an airplane."

"Boomer 30, thanks for the gas and the practice session," Kurfman transmitted to the tanker. "We'll be on our way now. Good night."

"Bronco 21, you're very welcome. By the way, tell your copilot he done good."

Troy felt good upon hearing the comment—his confidence soared.

Two more celestial navigation legs over the Pacific and a simulated bomb run on Los Angeles, and the crew wrapped up the night's activities.

Starting the descent from forty thousand feet into March AFB, Major Kurfman asked, "Troy, you wanna make the penetration and approach?"

"Yes, sir … I've got the airplane."

At about one hundred feet, Kurfman took over and landed the plane. "Troy, you did a good job of getting her down to approach altitude and intersecting the glide path," Kurfman said.

Troy was struck by the reduced visibility from the copilot's seat during the landing phase. He wondered if he'd ever be able to land the B-47 from the copilot's seat. Judging from what he had just seen, it looked to be almost impossible.

It had been nine hours since the crew's takeoff from March. Troy was impressed with how busy the entire crew had been throughout the flight, particularly the bomb-nav. None of the three had time to eat their flight lunches other than quickly nibbling on a few carrot sticks.

With the half-hour debriefing session over, Kurfman walked outside with Troy. "How about coming to the house for dinner tonight?" he asked.

"Thank you, sir, I'd like that."

As he drove back to the BOQ, the bright, early morning sun stung Troy's eyes. When he got to his room, Troy flopped on the bed, still in his sweaty flight suit, and fell into a deep, comatose sleep.

Chapter IV

JEAN KURFMAN OPENED THE door to a modest four-bedroom government house at March AFB.

"You must be Troy Bench. Allan told me you'd be coming for dinner. He just ran down to the base exchange to gas up the car. I'm Jean Kurfman," as she reached out to shake his hand.

Jean Kurfman was an attractive and charismatic woman in her late thirties, the mother of three girls. As wife of the chief pilot in the squadron, she was expected to play den mother to the other crew members' wives, a job she relished and excelled at. Expecting a more reserved person somewhat like her husband, Troy was pleasantly surprised.

"I'm pleased to meet you, Mrs. Kurfman."

"Troy, please call me Jean," she said as they walked into the kitchen. "What can I fix you to drink? I'm having a beer."

"A beer's fine."

Jean fumbled through several drawers for an opener. "Troy, I have to tell you that Allan is tickled to death to have you on his crew. He's always been fortunate to have outstanding people flying with him, but I'm going to tell you a secret: he's very impressed with you as an officer, as well as with your flying skills. And I'll tell you another secret." Jean found the opener she had been seeking. "My husband is not a man who's easily impressed."

"Thank you, ma'am—ah, Jean. I appreciate the encouragement." Troy gratefully took the opened beer she offered. "I felt like I was all elbows and knees up there today—or last night, I guess it was."

A knock at the front door interrupted their conversation. "Troy, could you get that, please? It's probably John and Betty Nale."

Allan Kurfman and John Nale had flown together in prop-driven B-50s and then transitioned as a crew into B-47 jet bombers. They were best friends, as were their wives. Their long friendship paid off when they were flying. It was almost as if one of them would breathe and the other would sense what he needed.

"Troy, have you recovered yet?" Major Nale asked as he entered the room.

"I feel fine, sir."

"Betty, this is the young man I was telling you about. He did a great job taking celestial shots for me last night and anticipating my every need up in the nose. Troy, I'd like you to meet my wife, Betty. Betty, this is Troy Bench."

Troy thought both women were very much alike: gregarious and outgoing; he liked them both immediately.

The evening was filled with much laughter and interesting stories about flying and families. Comfortably sharing stories from his life, Troy almost felt like he was spending time with his own family.

Arriving back in the BOQ later that night, Troy dialed Wendy's apartment in Tempe.

"Hello … " came a sleepy response.

"Hi, honey. I know it's late. Hope I didn't wake you."

Wendy's voice came to life. "Oh, Troy, I'm so glad you called. I was just dozing off. How did the flight go?"

Troy was pleased that Wendy had taken such an interest in his new flying job. He recounted the night refueling, taking celestial shots for Major Nale, and having dinner with the Kurfmans and Nales.

"You sound excited, honey. I'm glad it went well for you. I just wish I was there with you. I miss you so much."

"I know, honey. I miss you, too."

"You know, Troy, I have a long weekend coming up—Halloween, I think. How about me coming over? I can get a ride with Annabelle—she's driving out to see her family in Long Beach. We can then drive to Anaheim and get together with my parents. They want us to come out to the farm."

"I look forward to that, sweetie."

"Oh, and by the way, I met with my faculty advisor today. I have some great news to discuss with you, Troy."

"Honey, I'll call you tomorrow night after I finish at the squadron, and we'll finalize the arrangements. I love you so much, Wendy."

"I love you, too, Troy, and miss you terribly. Good night, my darling."

....

Wendy and Annabelle arrived at the March AFB O Club early in the evening after driving across the desert from Tempe. Troy invited Annabelle to join them for dinner at the club before she continued to Long Beach. A striking young woman with long, coal black hair, she had an inviting smile and a model's body.

Always with an eagle eye for beautiful ladies, Mark Denman, upon seeing Annabelle sitting with Troy and Wendy, got off his bar stool and strolled over to their table. Knowing Mark's penchant for beautiful women, Troy was not surprised to see his friend appear at their table after catching a glimpse of Annabelle.

"Hi, Mark, good to see you," Wendy said. "Mark, I'd like you to meet Annabelle DeLuca, my roommate at ASU. We're just about to order dinner; won't you join us?"

"Thanks, I will."

Throughout dinner, Mark and Annabelle virtually ignored Troy and Wendy as they carried on a nonstop, easygoing conversation, interspersed with frequent laughter. It appeared as if they had known each other for years.

After dinner, Annabelle excused herself. "This has been wonderful, but I better start my drive to Long Beach." She reminded Wendy that she would pick her up Sunday afternoon at the club for the drive back to Arizona. "You all have a great weekend," she said with a smile.

Before Annabelle turned to leave, Mark stopped her and they exchanged phone numbers.

"Wendy, why didn't you tell me you had a gorgeous roommate?" Mark asked as he watched Annabelle leave the club. "I've got to see that girl again. I'm in love."

"Mark, you're always in love," Wendy said with a wry smile. "Annabelle's not a love-'em-and leave-'em girl. You be careful with her, Mark."

"Oh, I shall … I shall," Mark said with a broad smile. "See you guys later." He turned and ambled back to the bar.

Troy and Wendy finished their meals and walked to their BOQ room. "The other night on the phone you said you met with your faculty advisor," Troy reminded Wendy. "What was that all about?"

Wendy squeezed his hand. "Oh, Troy, I almost forgot! Professor Morrison reviewed my transcript. I only need three electives to graduate. So, it looks like I can move to Riverside at the end of this semester. I'll pick up the electives at UCLA and graduate with my bachelor's from Arizona State in May. What do you think?"

"Wow, that's great!" Troy said. "I'll start looking for an apartment next week."

....

Troy had met Wendy's parents before but had never been to their farm. He looked forward to the visit.

It was just as Wendy had described: a large, rambling ranch-style structure on a sloping, grassy hill surrounded by trees. A smoothly graded dirt road bordered by wooden rail fences on either side led up the hill to the house. Wendy's parents were waiting on the wide porch that surrounded the house on three sides.

Her mom ran to the Corvette as it came to a stop. She hugged her daughter, and then with a broad smile, turned toward Troy and gave him a warm hug as well. "Welcome to our home, Troy."

Marge Hardt was a high-energy, animated woman in her mid-forties. She had one of those faces that smiled all over and made you want to smile back.

Wendy got out of the car and hugged her dad.

"Troy, welcome to our home," Dan Hardt said, extending his hand.

The Hardts had vacated their newly-renovated master bedroom, insisting that Troy and Wendy enjoy the early morning views it allowed. Marge Hardt had decorated their bed with cuddly stuffed animals from Wendy's childhood.

After lunch on the terraced patio that overlooked rows of citrus groves and vineyards, Dan asked Troy if he'd like a tour of the farm. Troy eagerly agreed and soon found himself in an aging, multicolored GMC pickup with balding tires, sitting alongside three energetic, slobbering Australian shepherds.

"Since Disney started building their entertainment park a few miles south of here, these beautiful orchards and neighboring farms are in danger of being squeezed out by developers buying up land for homes and shopping centers," Dan explained. "It's become a cliché: 'a farm today, a shopping center tomorrow.' I don't want to sell, but I'm afraid I may be forced to. It's sad because most of us around here homesteaded this land over thirty years ago. We nurtured it with our bare hands and our hearts and made it productive."

"That *is* sad," Troy said. "I've never seen a more

beautiful farm. It's like one of those rolling hills farms you see pictured on the upper fold of a calendar — it's real America. I can see why you're so proud of it, sir."

Wendy helped her mom prepare a delicious dinner of wild salmon complemented by their award-winning cabernet sauvignon and white Riesling wines. The after-dinner conversation soon turned to Troy and his flying job at March AFB. Dan and Marge asked whether the Strategic Air Command was really a deterrent in the Cold War.

"You know, a discussion about SAC can be pretty dull, but if you're really interested, I'll do my best to explain." Troy received encouragement from around the table but cautioned them to stop him if they had questions or he got too detailed."Back in the mid-1950s, the United States implemented a defense system known as Mutually Assured Destruction, most often referred to as MAD. It stated that an attack on any part of the United States by the Soviets or its satellites would result in an immediate and massive retaliatory attack on the Soviet Union.

"To ensure that the Soviets knew we were serious, some backbone was put into the policy — a percentage of the SAC bomber force was placed on twenty-four-hour alert. Fifteen minutes after a warning, B-47 and B-52 bombers loaded with nuclear weapons could be airborne and on their way to strike their assigned Soviet-block targets.

"Even as we speak, chances are that somewhere in the world a SAC aircrew is briefing an alert force commander on their route and target information. I brief my commander every time I go on alert out at March."

"Are the targets all within range of the bombers?" Dan asked, leaning forward with interest. "Do they have enough fuel to get back to their bases?"

Troy hesitated but decided it would not be a breach of security to answer Dan's questions honestly. "Unfortunately, without airborne tanker support, *some* of the SAC wartime targets are beyond range of a return flight. But all SAC aircrews know that their prime job is to get the weapon on the target and then concentrate on finding an appropriate landing field.

"When we carry a nuke," he cautioned, "we have a responsibility to guard against human failure. Under a system called 'positive control,' each bomber crew member must independently verify the go-code, or the mission becomes a no-go situation and the bomber returns. If the go-code authenticates, the crew is authorized to proceed and release the weapon. Only the president can authorize the release of a nuclear weapon."

Marge and Dan listened intently and at times interrupted Troy to ask questions.

"Under the SAC alert system, I'll be deployed for periods of one to three months to forward bases in Guam, Alaska, or England."

Troy noticed how attentive Wendy had been during the discussion. He'd never talked much with her about the SAC system. Acknowledging his glance, she reached across the table and squeezed his hand.

"Troy, you don't know how pleased we are that you enlightened us on your job," Dan said. "Marge and I understand what you do at March a whole lot better now, and we certainly feel more secure knowing how the SAC system works."

....

After a good night's rest and an early morning walk through the vineyards, Troy and Wendy were on their way back to Riverside. At noon, Annabelle met them in the O Club. Once again, Wendy and Troy said their good-byes, but knowing that Wendy would be moving soon to Riverside eased the pain a little.

Troy found it hard to get his mind back on flying and SAC, but by Tuesday morning things had changed. A special safety briefing ordered by Lieutenant Colonel Blauw for 10:00 AM quickly brought Troy's focus back to his job.

Chapter V

BOMBER CREWS HURRIED TO take their seats in the 64th Bomb Squadron briefing room. A dozen or more gray flight-planning tables and several dozen mismatched metal folding chairs dominated the austere decor of the room. A hand-painted squadron emblem dangled loosely from the front of the scarred plywood lectern. The room reminded Troy of briefing rooms he'd seen in old World War II movies.

Kurfman, Nale, and Troy found seats up front. "Troy, do you know the purpose of this briefing?" Kurfman asked.

"I know SAC had some recent B-47 accidents. I assume that's what it's about."

"That's right, and unfortunately six lives were lost in those accidents. Colonel Blauw asked me to help out with the briefing this morning." Kurfman handed Troy a stack of slides. "I'd like you to flip these graphics for me later. They're in order."

"Yes, sir, glad to."

"Officers, a-ten-hut!" barked a lieutenant standing at the rear of the room.

Sixty crew members jumped to attention as Lieutenant Colonel Blauw walked swiftly to the podium. "Gentlemen, be seated."

Dressed in a flying suit, Blauw appeared tense and serious. "Those of you standing in the back of the room, drag a chair in. This may take a while."

After everyone was seated, Blauw continued. "You've all read the preliminary reports on the landing accidents last week at Schilling and Dyess Air Bases. These accidents were, in my opinion, preventable. Based on early reports, it appears both were the result of fatigued crews who made bad choices during the landing phase. Six precious lives and millions of dollars have been lost as a result.

"In both cases, the crews had completed nine-hour-long, all-night missions, landing at sunup. Crew members had been awake continuously for almost twenty-four hours. In one case, the aircraft commander had spent the previous day painting his house. In the other, both pilots spent most of the day doing yard work and baby-sitting. None of the crew members, as required by SAC regs, received his mandatory twelve hours of crew rest before the flight.

"And I just received more bad news. An hour ago, we got word from Lieutenant General Oman at 15th

Air Force that another B-47 crashed early this morning—this one at Davis-Monthan. The crew plowed into a 9,500-foot mountain thirty miles south of the base. All three airmen died on impact. From what we know now—and this is preliminary info only—this aircrew had also been up for almost twenty-four hours. Our best guess is that they misread the ten-thousand-foot needle on their altimeters and started their jet penetration ten thousand feet below the prescribed altitude over Tucson."

Noise in the outside hallway momentarily distracted Colonel Blauw. Looking toward the back of the room, he ordered, "Lieutenant, close that door and lock it."

Blauw returned his focus to the group and took a deep breath. "Gentlemen, I'm going to speak frankly and from my gut. I'm telling you right here and now that I will not put up with any violation of crew rest regulations. I want each of you to understand that loud and clear."

Pausing, Blauw took several steps toward the front of the podium and stared intently at his audience. He spoke slowly but with command. "Any of you violating these regulations will lose his job. I absolutely promise you, here and now, that you'll be flying a goddamn trash hauler for the rest of your Air Force career. Is that crystal clear?"

No one moved as the men stared straight ahead.

Blauw continued to speak with deliberation. "The squadron scheduler programs each of you with an ample amount of crew rest time prior to a mission. I expect that time to be utilized in crew rest, not doing household chores or playing golf. I'm well aware that most of you have children at home. You also have wives who expect you to work around the house during your off-duty time. I can empathize with that. But you're going to have to explain to your wives that you'll do those chores at another time—*not* during the twelve hours preceding an all-night mission."

Stepping off the platform and moving down the aisle, Blauw peered at each flier, seeming to search for signs that he had made his point. His voice morphed into a somewhat more compassionate tone. "I want you bastards alive. As squadron commander, my job is to train you and keep you alive so that if we're ordered to fly a nuclear combat mission against the Soviets, we'll be ready. That's why we're here, goddammit—and don't ever forget that."

Troy sensed the tense uneasiness in the room. He was impressed with how Colonel Blauw had handled the briefing.

Stepping back onto the platform, Blauw took on a more instructive tenor. "Everyone in this room has between five hundred and four thousand flying hours, and a lot of you have some tough combat missions under your belts from two wars. You're professionals; you've all been doing this for a while. There's absolutely no reason on God's Earth that you can't stay alert and focus your attention for the final twenty minutes during the approach-and-landing phase of this very demanding airplane.

"A lot of pilots say that landing this plane is more akin to a controlled crash than to a landing. We know that the B-47, with its bicycle landing gear, its relatively high approach speed and low drag all combine to make it damned unforgiving if it's not handled properly—the boneyard at Davis-Monthan is littered with evidence of that. And we know you can get into serious trouble if you touch down on your forward main gear first, throwing you into a lateral porpoising situation that might be unrecoverable. Applying full power and initiating a go-around may be the only thing that can save your ass. And lastly, each of us is well aware how weary pilots and crew members can misread and misinterpret instruments."

Blauw raised his voice to a higher pitch and thumped the lectern for emphasis. "Frankly, I don't care how goddamn tired you feel when you're on the final approach-and-landing phase of your mission. Rub your eyes, bang your head on the side of the canopy, and go to 100 percent oxygen. Do whatever it goddamned takes to get your concentration and focus to a fine point for your jet penetration and landing."

Blauw peered intently at his audience. "I don't

want to be the guy who has to notify your family that you won't be coming home."

Blauw's words echoed through the silent room. His voice softened. "Are there any questions about what I've said and what I expect from you?"

The men remained quiet. After waiting a few seconds, Blauw nodded. "Okay, if there aren't any questions, Major Kurfman will discuss crew-rest regs with you and review jet penetrations, landings, and touchdown procedures."

Blauw took a seat in the front row.

For the next twenty minutes, Kurfman detailed SAC crew-rest regs and discussed the twenty-four-hour after-accident reports from Schilling and Dyess. He then went into great detail on landing and go-around procedures and timing for deployment of the brake chute.

Kurfman then summarized. "Gentlemen, these crews made boneheaded mistakes. They'd been awake for at least twenty-four hours at the time of the accidents, and fatigue clouded their judgment. Under normal circumstances and with proper crew rest, chances are they would not have made these deadly mistakes. Nine crew members would be alive today."

Kurfman concluded the briefing, and the crews filed out of the room in silence. Troy's mind raced as he thought about the loss of lives due to a split-second lapse in judgment.

Troy went directly to the squadron library where B-47 tech orders were kept. He had an idea. His mind had focused on the predescent and landing checklists. As he had guessed, the altimeter crosscheck involved only the copilot and the aircraft commander; the bomb-nav was not included in the verification. There had to be a reason for that, but he found none. Could it possibly be just an oversight? Maybe a third crew member crosschecking the altimeter could have saved the crew at Davis-Monthan.

The following morning Troy approached Major Kurfman with his idea. "Sir, I know I'm the five-hundred-hour pilot that Colonel Blauw was talking about, and I know I'm the new guy on the block. But I think I may have found something that crews can do to provide an extra layer of safety during jet penetrations."

"What is it, Troy?" Kurfman asked with interest. "Sometimes we miss the forest for the trees, or however that goes. Maybe we're too close to the problem. Either way, I'm open to suggestions."

"Sir, what if we got the bomb-nav involved in the crosschecks, starting with the predescent checklist and on down to final approach? Wouldn't three heads be better than one or two? The bomb-navs that I've met are technically oriented and focused and could easily provide that third layer of safety. Through an oral challenge-and-response, each crew member would verify the position of the three altimeter needles, particularly the ten-thousand-foot needle, before starting the penetration and at critical points during the descent. As it's done now, the pilots simply verify the altitudes silently, and more often than not, the readings are never coordinated."

"Makes sense to me, Troy. Let me grab John Nale, and we'll go talk with Colonel Blauw about it."

....

"Damn, you guys come up with some of the strangest things," Blauw said. "Why didn't someone think of this before? What do *you* think about the idea, John?"

John Nale said that he had always accomplished the crosscheck silently but agreed that an oral challenge-and-response crosscheck with the pilots could save lives. "I like the idea, sir."

"Okay, Allan," Blauw said, "you guys get a briefing together along with a written proposal, and I'll grease the skids at wing-and-division level. Some people may think this proposal is overkill, but dammit, if we can save one airman's life it'll be worth it."

Blauw turned to Troy. "Bench, I appreciate your unconventional thinking. Good work." Upon leaving the squadron, Troy checked the crew scheduling board and found that he was on the next day's flying schedule. This was followed by four days of twenty-four-hour alert duty over the weekend. *Welcome to SAC, Troy,* he thought.

Chapter VI

THREE HOURS BEFORE MAJOR Jim Gibson and his B-47 crew were to depart on an eight-hour night mission, his copilot, Bill Candee, called in sick. Troy was in OPS when Gibson received the call.

"Hey, Troy, you want to play copilot for me tonight?" Gibson asked.

"Yes, sir, I do. Just give me five minutes." Troy was beginning to enjoy flying the high-performance silver bird, and he grabbed every opportunity to build up his flying time. After changing into a flying suit, he completed a hasty review of the aircraft performance data that Lieutenant Candee had prepared the day before. He also called Wendy to let her know he'd be home late. The mission was a check ride for Gibson's bomb-nav, Captain Joe Mangino. Troy had met Major Gibson and Captain Mangino a few days before when they had shared the same alert cycle, and he'd worked with Major Paul Olivier, Mangino's check-ride examiner in the squadron.

The setting sun cast its final shadows over the California coastline as Gibson lined up on runway three-two at March AFB. With the brakes released, the ninety-ton B-47 rumbled down the runway and gracefully lifted into the air at 160 knots. Troy was fascinated with how the 116-foot swept wings of the big bomber flexed upward as much as eight feet during the takeoff roll, eagerly trying to fly before the rest of the airplane was ready.

Within minutes they had climbed through twenty thousand feet into the inky darkness of the Pacific sky, preparing to start a two-hour nighttime celestial navigation leg. Troy turned down the white cockpit lights and turned up the red instrument and cabin lights so his eyes could adapt to the darkness and allow him to take celestial shots for Mangino. The low-intensity lighting bathed the cockpit in a red glow, projecting a sense of calm.

Dragging a long oxygen hose behind him, Troy looked down to his left toward the narrow crawl-way to see Major Olivier on his hands and knees, crawling toward the nose of the airplane where he could evaluate Mangino's work. Olivier's tortured facial expression showed how uncomfortable he was, with his frame ensconced on a small fiberglass box, a chest-pack parachute stowed beside him. Troy felt empathy for the major and guessed that the fourth-man position in the B-47 had to have been a design afterthought. Because the fourth man did not have an ejection seat, the escape plan called for him to release the pressure door at the entryway and bail out, or go through the open space created after the downward ejection of the bomb-nav. Neither of these emergency exits enjoyed a high success rate.

At the start of the celestial navigation leg, Troy called over the interphone. "Hey, Joe, what heavenly bodies do you want me to shoot for you tonight?"

"How about Deneb, Altair, and Venus? They should give me a good celestial fix."

With the periscopic sextant inserted through the canopy outlet above his head, Troy placed the instrument crosshairs on each celestial body, averaging the declination of the body over a two-minute period. Mangino then applied a series of computations to each reading that resulted in a line of position that he plotted on his chart. Three celestial lines formed a tight triangle, the center of which fixed the position of the aircraft—pretty much the same method that Columbus used several hundred years earlier, only now with more expensive and sophisticated instruments. Troy guessed that in a few years a star tracker and a computer would do this work automatically, but for now the bomb-nav and copilot shared the tedious, painstaking job.

After completing the two-hour overwater celestial leg, Mangino called back to Troy. "Those were great celestial shots. I came in with a three-miler. Thanks!"

Following simulated-radar bomb runs on San Francisco and Denver, the crew prepared for the low-level phase of the mission. This combat tactic called for the B-47 crew to descend at high speed, level off four hundred feet above the ground, perform evasive maneuvers for an hour at 425 knots, and terminate with a high-speed simulated bomb run. The crew would use these tactics against many of their wartime Soviet targets.

They were scheduled to fly the Diablo route in northern New Mexico, which was more difficult than most low-levels. Situated in the midst of rugged terrain and threatening mountain peaks, it demanded absolute concentration and focus by every crew member. Being off course by a couple of miles or an altitude error of a few hundred feet could spell disaster.

This wasn't Troy's first low-level. He had flown a high-speed, low-level night route with Kurfman's crew the previous week.

Gibson asked Troy to make the entry call. "Albuquerque Center, this is Disco Three-eight. Request permission to enter Diablo low-level."

"Roger, Disco Three-eight, you're cleared into Diablo. Notify us at designated checkpoints and at exit."

Major Gibson pushed the nose over and started

down at four hundred knots. The crew members crosschecked airspeed and altitude at thousand-foot increments until leveling off four hundred feet above the ground south of Cortez, Colorado. The moonlit night silhouetted the jagged peaks of the Ute Mountains jutting upward on both sides of the bomber. Two altitude changes were required before reaching the first turning point near Farmington, New Mexico. As Gibson advanced the throttles for the first step climb of nineteen hundred feet, the aircraft shuddered and the sky on the right side of the airplane lit up like a Roman candle.

"Troy, what the hell was that? What's going on out there?" Gibson called over the interphone as he leveled the airplane and engaged the autopilot.

"Number six is on fire. We need to shut it down," Troy responded.

Gibson pulled the number-six throttle back and tripped the fuel cutoff switch, but the fire continued to burn.

Advancing the remaining throttles to climb power, Gibson said, "I'm gonna get some altitude between us and the ground. Call Albuquerque and advise 'em of our situation. Tell 'em we're aborting Diablo and climbing to two-six thousand!"

"Roger, sir. Albuquerque has cleared us to twenty-six thousand and asked that we keep them advised."

"Troy, from what I can see it looks like the fire's burning into the wing. Can you see it any clearer?"

"I'm not sure the wing is burning, Major. It might just be clouds reflecting off the engine fire."

In a commanding voice, Gibson announced, "Okay, crew, listen up. Prepare to bail out, but do *not* go until I give the order. I say again, *do not go* until I give the order."

Looking down at the crawlway, Troy saw Major Olivier holding a chest-pack chute, preparing for bailout through the bomb-nav hatch, if necessary. To his right, he saw red and blue flames streaming fifty to one hundred feet behind the wing.

"Troy, it doesn't look to me like that fire's going out. I'm concerned that it's burned into the wing and could explode anytime. What do you think?"

"I agree," Troy said. "I'll call Albuquerque Center with a Mayday and advise them that we're preparing to bail out." Troy was impressed by the professionalism of everyone on the airplane; there was no panic.

Moments later, the fire still showed no sign of extinguishing. Major Gibson engaged the autopilot, turned on the emergency alarm bell, and reluctantly gave the order: *"Bail out! Bail out! Bail out!"*

As the bomb-nav, Mangino ejected first and with success. The aftereffects of explosive decompression at twenty-six thousand feet enveloped the crew compartment: a blizzard of papers, checklists, and debris swirled around the darkened and momentarily fog-filled cockpit. What had been a comfortable environment seconds before had suddenly exploded into a dark and frigid wind tunnel. The noise was deafening, and the temperature plummeted almost one hundred degrees. A four-hundred-knot blast of air rasped Troy's body and dulled his senses. Even with his mask tightened, breathing in the rarified atmosphere became difficult. Water vapor forming in his soft body tissues caused his internal organs to swell and expand to twice their size.

As part of the pilot's ejection sequence, the aircraft canopy automatically blew off, creating even more swirling debris. The wind stream blasting through the cockpit stung Troy's face and peeled back his eyelids. Assuming Troy had ejected, Major Gibson squeezed his ejection-seat triggers and yanked up on the handles, but his seat didn't fire. He disconnected from the seat and crawled down with his backpack parachute to the open hatch left from the bomb-nav's downward ejection. Crouching into a ball, he tumbled through the dark abyss.

Troy squeezed his ejection seat handles, but his seat also failed to fire. He tried again; still nothing happened. Disconnecting from his seat, he stepped down into the darkened aisle and began crawling on his hands and knees over debris toward the open bomb-nav hatch. As he did, he bumped into some-

thing and realized it was Major Olivier lying prostrate in the crawlway.

Troy felt around for Olivier's parachute but found
none. He assumed that the explosive decompression
had blown Olivier into the bulkhead and rendered
him unconscious. Olivier appeared pale and lifeless.
As Troy tightened the major's oxygen mask, a stream
of partially frozen blood oozed from Olivier's forehead. Troy grabbed a wad of paper napkins from a
nearby flight lunch and jammed them between the
unconscious examiner's helmet and forehead to slow
the bleeding.

As he did so, Troy began to feel light-headed and
his breathing quickened. He couldn't think clearly
and realized he was becoming hypoxic. He needed
to get back in his seat and transfer from the small
parachute bailout oxygen bottle to the main aircraft
oxygen system. Clawing his way up into the seat, he
reconnected to 100-percent oxygen under pressure,
and his head became immediately clearer.

As Troy turned toward the right wing to check the
fire, the wind stream whipped his head and shoulder violently to the right, almost ripping off his helmet, and slammed him against the back of the seat.
He lowered his ejection seat as far as it would go and
crouched down to avoid the main impact of the wind-
blast. The subfreezing temperature was beginning to
take its toll on his mind and body. Troy knew he had

to stay focused; he couldn't let his mind wander. Experiencing numbness in his hands, he snugged up his gloves and flexed his fingers to keep them from freezing.

Thoughts of every sort bombarded his mind. *What if the major is dead or dying? Am I wasting my time trying to keep this airplane aloft? Should I save my own skin?* Glancing down at Olivier, the thoughts were dispelled. Troy knew that he had to try and save him. He couldn't live with himself if he didn't try.

First, he had to get to a lower altitude with more oxygen if he were going to save either of them. Troy unlocked and reengaged the steering column, which had automatically stowed in the forward position as part of the pilot's ejection sequence. With the airplane still on autopilot, he lowered the nose and dived the aircraft at 350 knots. He leveled off at fifteen thousand feet, and then set the throttles as best he could to maintain 280 knots. Squinting downward through swollen eyes, he thought he saw Major Olivier move.

After several attempts, he managed to switch the radios to an emergency UHF frequency. Troy spoke as clearly and distinctly as he could: "*Mayday! Mayday!* This is Disco Three-eight. I'm flying an Air Force B-47 without a canopy. I'm at fifteen thousand feet somewhere over northern New Mexico. I have a fire on my number-six engine. My pilot and bomb-nav have bailed out. I have an unconscious crew member onboard without a parachute. Does anyone read me, over?"

A cacophony of voices responded. "Disco Three-eight, this is Albuquerque Center reading you loud and clear. Squawk your call sign for positive ID. Roger, Three-eight, we have you on radar thirty miles south of Farmington, New Mexico. Climb immediately to one-eight thousand feet to clear terrain in your vicinity. How can we help?"

"Roger, Albuquerque, I'm climbing to eighteen. Notify March Air Force Base Command Post of my situation. And I need a vector to March."

Troy could see that Major Olivier had plugged back into the aircraft communication system. Groggy but coherent, Olivier asked how he could help. Troy asked him to stay on interphone, and that he may need him later.

"Disco Three-eight, this is Albuquerque. Turn heading two-five-zero, maintain one-eight thousand. March Command Post wants you to switch to the emergency high-frequency channel."

"Negative! Negative! Albuquerque. I'm having trouble changing radio channels—I'm not taking a chance of losing my lifeline. Patch March through on this frequency. And Albuquerque, ask them to get Colonel Kurfman into the command post."

Troy was calm and focused. For the moment, he felt in control. He was having some difficulty breathing, but his biggest nemesis was the frigid cold. Each passing minute sapped more of his strength.

"Disco Three-eight, this is Albuquerque. The command post wants to know the status of the fire on your number six." Troy had been so busy he hadn't looked in that direction for some time. He was surprised to see that the fire must have extinguished itself during the dive.

"The engine fire appears to be out, Albuquerque."

....

Colonel Kurfman raced to the command post, stunned by what he had heard on his home phone, his mind tangled in thoughts of how to handle the situation. No one had ever landed the huge bomber from the backseat without a pilot in front, much less at night, with the canopy off, on just five engines, and with a young pilot who had little more than five hundred flying hours. But Kurfman knew that if anyone could pull it off, Troy Bench might be able to.

Driving down near-empty base streets in his Austin Healey, Kurfman focused on the countless details and cautions he needed to pass on to Troy. He knew that if he was going to get Troy on the ground, he had to stay calm himself and provide short and precise instructions. Above all, he had to project absolute confidence in all of his communication.

....

"Disco Three-eight, this is Albuquerque. We're handing you off to Phoenix Center. Remain on this frequency. We'll stand by to ensure you make contact with Phoenix. And, sir … we wish you luck."

"Disco Three-eight, this is Phoenix Center. We have a Colonel Kurfman patched through on this freq. Go ahead, Colonel."

"Troy, this is Colonel Kurfman. Can you hear me?"

"I can barely hear you, Colonel. It's awful noisy."

"Troy, SAC has directed that you put the airplane in a descent and point it out over the Pacific. They want you and Major Olivier to bail out through the bomb-nav hatch near Edwards Air Force Base. Do you understand?"

"Can't do that, Colonel. Major Olivier doesn't have a chute—it must have blown out during explosive decompression. I have to land this thing; I don't have a choice. And, Colonel … I really need you to guide me down. Can you help me, sir?"

Kurfman sensed some fear in Troy's voice, but he also detected strength and confidence.

"Roger, Troy." Kurfman tried to sound reassuring. "We'll do it together."

....

At SAC headquarters in Omaha, General Strong was awakened by a phone call from his aide, Colonel Bill Murphy, who informed him of the situation.

"Good Lord, Bill, no one's ever attempted this in a B-47!" the general blurted out. "What's the pilot's name, and what's his experience?"

"Lieutenant Troy Bench, sir, and he's got something like five hundred total flying hours. The 22nd Bomb Wing people tell me he's quite an exceptional young man. The fourth man doesn't have a chute, and Bench is determined to land the bomber. On the plus side, General, we have one of the finest B-47 instructor pilots in SAC, Lieutenant Colonel Allan Kurfman, talking him down."

"Bill, make damn sure our SAC headquarters guys don't interfere. I don't want any of my staff people mucking this up. I'm on my way to the command post now. And, Bill, make arrangements to land him at Edwards Air Force Base. They've got a longer and wider runway with more safety features than March."

Troy had no idea that most every airplane flying that night was listening silently to his unfolding drama. Several media stations in the Los Angeles area had learned of the incident and were badgering the Air Force to provide information for their late-night newscasts. They were told to stand by, but that didn't keep them from preemptively broadcasting, "A huge Strategic Air Command jet bomber, possibly carrying a nuclear weapon and five or six crew members onboard, is lost and on fire somewhere over New Mexico. The Air Force will neither confirm nor deny this information."

....

"Disco Three-eight, this is Kurfman. Troy, we've calculated your weight and balance data. You need to transfer fifteen hundred pounds of fuel from your aft-main tank, *now*. This will put your center of gravity within limits for landing. And, Troy, we're landing you at Edwards Air Force Base on a three-mile-long runway."

"Colonel, the air blast has swelled my eyes almost shut, and I think it's burned 'em pretty bad. I can't see much more than images. I'm really having trouble reading my instruments, and the noise level is horrendous."

Troy yanked at the nylon straps on his oxygen mask and helmet, wrenching the helmet and earphones even tighter to his head. "I'm having a problem hearing you, Colonel, even with the volume full up. And the only way I can estimate airspeed is by feeling the position of the throttles with my gloved hand—and that can't be real accurate."

"Roger, Troy. Use whatever works for you. What's Major Olivier's condition?"

"He's conscious but groggy. Think the bleeding has stopped."

"Troy, don't be alarmed when you see lights off your wing. We've scrambled two F-86 fighters from

Edwards. They're on their way to check over your airplane for damage and crosscheck your airspeeds, altitudes, and headings. They'll stay with you until you land."

"Colonel, how much farther have I got to go? I'm having trouble moving my hands, and my legs feel like they're in a block of ice. I hope I can use the rudders. It's so-o-o damn cold … I don't know how much longer I can do this, Colonel."

Kurfman knew he had to keep Troy engaged in dialogue and keep him busy; he had detected some slurred speech. Although Troy had youth on his side, Kurfman sensed that Troy was fading as each minute ticked away.

"Troy, you're eighteen minutes from touchdown at Edwards. You're doing just fine. I want you to descend to ten thousand feet now. Keep your airspeed around 190—do not go below 170. And Troy, in about eight minutes, Edwards Ground-Controlled Approach will take over. I'll also be standing by on that frequency."

"Roger, Colonel. I think I'm at ten thousand, and I think my escort has arrived."

"Troy, the F-86 pilots have checked you over and advised us that they see no damage to your control surfaces. I want you to extend your gear and flaps, *now*. Keep your airspeed between 170 and 180.

"Troy, descend *now* to five thousand feet and turn

to heading two-seven-zero. Your fighter escort says that your gear is down and appears locked, and your airspeed is 178. Troy, you're doing just fine. Another six minutes and you'll be on the ground."

"Colonel, this is only my fourth backseat landing in this airplane. Hope I'm not being graded."

"You are, and the grade's going to be outstanding." Kurfman's voice was reassuring. "Troy, GCA will take over now. You'll be landing on runway two-three, left, at Edwards. It's fifteen thousand feet long and three hundred feet wide, so you've got plenty of room. The field elevation is 2,300 feet. The F-86s will monitor your airspeed all the way down. Your best-flare speed is 134 knots. I'll be staying with you on this freq. You're doing just fine, Troy. Good luck."

"Disco Three-eight, this is Edwards GCA. How do you read?"

"I can barely hear you, GCA."

"Roger, Three-eight, you need not acknowledge further transmissions. Descend now to three thousand feet ... Turn heading two-three-five ... You're on course ... You're a little high on glide path ... Your airspeed should be 154 knots ... You're two miles from the end of the runway ... You're still high on glide path and ten knots fast ... You're on course ... Decrease your airspeed, you're still high on glide path ... You're forty feet above glide path and fifteen knots fast."

"Troy, this is Kurfman. Pull your throttles back two inches and lower your nose, *now*."

"Three-eight, you're high and fast … You're over the end of the runway … Take over visually and land."

Troy yanked the throttles back to idle and held the airplane at what he prayed was the proper aircraft attitude. He couldn't afford to touch down on the forward main gear first and risk a dangerous porpoise. After what seemed a lifetime, he felt the aft gear touch. He yanked on the brake chute handle, and the chute deployed, slowing the aircraft. The forward main gear dropped to the runway with a tremendous thud, and the aircraft veered left. Troy stomped on the brakes and mashed in some right rudder. The weaving and screeching bomber finally came to rest two thousand feet from the end of the runway.

A multitude of emergency vehicles surrounded the bomber, their rotating red and blue lights creating a blurred and eerie sensation. Troy shut down the remaining five engines and flipped every switch he could see or feel to the OFF position.

It was two minutes past midnight. Troy took a deep breath and glanced down at Major Olivier, who smiled weakly and reached his right hand up to slap Troy's boot and mouthed "thank you."

Reaching down to unbuckle his lap belt, Troy was shocked to discover that it had never been buckled.

Chapter VII

BECAUSE THE PLANE'S ENTRY door was jammed, a cherry-picker crane extracted Troy and Major Olivier through the pilot's canopy opening. Ambulances whisked them to the Edwards AFB hospital.

Pilots and maintenance personnel gazed in disbelief at the remains of Disco Three-eight, now looking like a badly wounded giant vertebrate sprawled on the tarmac. A charred J-47 engine dangled from its pedestal. A portion of the right wing tip was burned off. The pilot's compartment, once covered by a Plexiglas canopy, looked like an apparition. A large open space in the forward underbelly of the aircraft that once housed the platform for the bomb-nav ejection seat appeared eerily unnatural. An old-time Edwards test pilot summed it up best: "I don't know how anyone could taxi that hulk, much less fly the son of a bitch for two hours."

Wendy finally picked up the phone after several long rings, answering sleepily.

"Wendy, this is Jack Blauw. I apologize for waking you at this hour, but I wanted to tell you that Troy won't be home; he landed at Edwards Air Force Base tonight. I also want to let you know that for the last few hours your husband single-handedly flew a badly crippled airplane under extreme conditions and landed it at Edwards."

Anxiously, Wendy asked, "Colonel, is he okay?"

"He's undergoing medical treatment at the Edwards hospital now. Mrs. Blauw and I will pick you up in ten minutes and drive you to the hospital."

During the drive, Blauw arranged a radio telephone hookup from his staff car. Handing the radiophone to Wendy, he explained how to use the talk-and-receive buttons. Then he connected her with Troy.

"Honey, Colonel Blauw told me a little about what you did tonight. He says you're a true hero. Are you okay?" Wendy asked.

"I'm just fine. And I'm no hero. I *had* to stay with the airplane—I didn't have a choice. But I need to warn you, I'm not going to win any beauty contests for a while. My face is pretty beat up with first- and second-degree burns. Oh, and I'm temporarily blind. Other than that I'm just fine. I *am* really tired, though. Honey, could you call my parents before they hear about this from someone else?"

"I'll do that right away, darling. This radiophone I'm using has a lot of static. I'm having a hard time understanding you. Colonel Blauw says we'll be there in a half hour. Can't wait to see you, my darling."

"I need to get off the phone, too, Wendy. General Strong is holding for me on the other line. Can you believe a four-star general wants to talk with me? God, I hope he's not upset. I love you, sweetie. Bye."

Troy switched to the other line to speak with General Strong.

"Lieutenant Bench, this is General Strong. Hope you can hear me okay. I've just finished talking with your doctors. They don't expect any permanent medical problems from your injuries. I've told them that whatever you need in the way of medical treatment you're to receive, even if it means taking you to the UCLA Medical Center. Lieutenant, what you did tonight took a lot of courage and some damned exceptional flying.

"And I also want to thank you for saving Major Paul Olivier's life. Major Olivier was my special assistant for two years before going back to a flying job.

"By the way, Lieutenant, I just received an update on Major Gibson and Captain Mangino. They've been picked up in New Mexico in good condition."

"I'm really glad to hear that, General."

"Lieutenant Bench, I'm awarding you the Distinguished Flying Cross for what you did. You certainly earned it."

"Thank you, sir. But I have to credit some very dedicated people on the ground for helping me. And I also had a whole bunch of luck going for me."

"I understand all that, Lieutenant, but there aren't many pilots I know who could have pulled off what you did. I'm extending an invitation for you and your wife, and any family members you want to bring, to come to Omaha once you feel up to it. We'll do a formal presentation of your DFC.

"Thank you, sir, I look forward to it."

"And, Lieutenant, I might as well forewarn you that by this evening, through the magic of television, most everyone in America will have heard about what you did. You might as well prepare yourself for a media onslaught. We'll do our best to keep the buzzards away, but some are bound to get through. Get some rest, Lieutenant. We'll talk more when you get to Omaha."

"Yes, sir. Thank you, General."

The Air Force Office of Information at March issued a short press release at 2:00 AM: A Strategic Air Command B-47 Stratojet bomber from the 22nd Bomb Wing at March AFB, California, landed safely at Edwards AFB around midnight following an in-flight emergency. The aircraft carried a crew of four. Two crewmen bailed out of the stricken bomber near Farmington, New Mexico. Both were picked up by local authorities and are being treated for minor injuries in the Farmington hospital. The two crewmen who landed the aircraft are in the Edwards AFB hospital with non-life-threatening injuries. No bombs were onboard the airplane. The crew members' names are being withheld pending notification. A press conference is scheduled at the March AFB Theater for 1:00 PM today.

....

Wendy giggled when she laid eyes on Troy in his hospital bed, all swathed in bandages. "Honey, you look like a mummy. Do you hurt badly?"

"They've got me so doped up on painkillers I don't feel a thing. Honey, can you believe General Strong awarded me a DFC? And he's invited you … and our … families to … Omaha for a … presentation … " Troy's soft murmuring trailed off. He felt like heavy weights were pressing down on his eyelids..

"Darling, go to sleep. I'll be here when you wake up," Wendy whispered as she kissed an unbandaged spot on his forehead.

A nurse dragged in an elevated lounge chair for her. With Wendy holding Troy's hand, they slept soundly for the next several hours.

....

Within a week, Troy's injuries had healed enough

for him to be transferred to the March AFB hospital. He wasn't prepared for what took place as the ambulance drove through the March entrance. About a hundred wives, children, and fellow airmen of all ranks lined the entry road, waving, cheering, and holding up welcoming signs as the ambulance proceeded slowly toward the hospital. Tears stung Troy's still-swollen eyes as he viewed the overwhelming welcome through thick, dark glasses. He said a prayer, thanking God that everything had turned out the way it had.

An investigation board convened within days of the accident. It didn't take them long to conclude that Major Gibson had made the correct decision to bail out the crew when he determined that the fire had burned into the wing and could not be extinguished. The board praised Troy's actions in staying with the crippled bomber once he discovered that Major Olivier was incapacitated.

....

Three weeks after the incident, a KC-135 tanker flew the Bench family and Wendy's parents to Omaha for a presentation ceremony. They were given a personalized tour of the public part of the supersecret SAC headquarters facility and the central war room with its backlit, floor-to-ceiling wall charts, covered for security. A short, informal social gathering followed the presentation ceremony in General Strong's office.

General Strong then excused the others, and he

and Troy sat down in his office. The general asked what Troy's goals were. Troy hesitated for a moment, and then blurted out that he had always wanted to fly fighters.

"I can't do that for you right now, Lieutenant. But what I will do is place a memo in your personnel jacket, recommending that you be transferred to fighters as soon as our bomber personnel situation improves.

"This morning, I called your wing commander at March and recommended that you be given your own B-47 crew. Normally you'd need twice the flying hours you have to become an aircraft commander, but you've proved to me that you have the maturity and leadership to command a SAC bomber crew. I wish you luck, Lieutenant. And God bless you for what you did."

"Thank you, General Strong," Troy said, standing to shake the general's hand. "I won't let you down."

"I know you won't, Lieutenant."

Following the ceremony, they boarded a KC-135 for the flight back to March. Troy's father expressed his personal feelings during the return flight to March. "Troy, I came to America more than thirty years ago with no job and no money. I could never have imagined that I would someday fly in a big government airplane and be given a personal tour of one of the most secret buildings in this great country. Did you see how they treated me? Like a king, Troy—just like a king!"

"Yes, I know, Papa, and you deserved it." Seeing

his father's damp eyes and sensing his pride, Troy's own eyes filled with tears."Troy, generals came up to me and shook my hand," his father said huskily. "Generals, Troy. They thanked *me*, as a father. Just wait till I tell the guys at the Smoke House about all of this. They're not gonna believe where I've been."

At that moment, Troy reached across the two seats and embraced his parents tightly. Backing off and looking into their eyes, he whispered, "I'm so proud that you're my parents. *Thank you.* Thank you for what you've given me. I love you both so much."

....

The Air Force information people insisted that Troy make at least a few guest appearances on national television and radio shows. He reluctantly agreed and appeared briefly on two nationally televised morning shows in New York City and three in the Los Angeles area.

Troy couldn't wait to get back to work. The wing had given him six weeks to get his new bomber crew up to combat-ready status. A crisis between the Soviets, Cuba, and the United States was brewing, and the wing needed to become fully manned and combat ready.

Chapter VIII

THE WEEK AFTER RETURNING from Omaha, Troy felt well enough to get back to work. As he entered the squadron, he passed Colonel Blauw in the hallway. "Troy, come into my office. We need to talk."

As Blauw shut the office door behind them, he asked how Troy was feeling. "Have you recovered enough to get back to work?"

"Yes, sir, I'm ready," Troy said eagerly. "The flight surgeon cleared me for duty this morning."

"Good," Blauw said. "I've got a problem that maybe you can help me with. I'm trying to put a crew together for you, but I don't have any lieutenant bomb-navs. I think I may have found a fix, though. Major Gibson has asked to be taken off a crew so that he can go back to the intelligence business. He's being transferred to the wing staff next week. That leaves his bomb-nav, Captain Joe Mangino, and his copilot, Lieutenant Bill Candee, without an aircraft commander. I've talked with both of them, and they'd be happy to fly with you. They're fine airmen, and I think the three of you would make a good fit. What do you think?"

"Sir, I'd love to fly with 'em. They're both fine officers and airmen."

"You'll be getting a well-qualified bomb-nav in Mangino, even though he outranks you. "And you know how important the bomb-nav is on a B-47—he can make or break the crew. And Bill Candee is an experienced copilot who should be getting his own crew within a year.

Troy nodded in understanding.

"Okay, then, it's settled. I'll submit your new crew to SAC for approval. Your crew number will be N-38, non-combat ready," Blauw said. "Now, Lieutenant, I want to shift gears and give you a little heads-up. There may be some resentment and backlash toward you among copilots who outrank you and have more flying time than you. And there could even be a few aircraft commanders who think you moved up too fast. I bring this up because it's something you may have to deal with along the way."

"Thank you, sir. I appreciate your confidence in me, and I'll stay alert to the potential problem."

Troy hurried home to tell Wendy the good news. Since the crew would be spending a lot of time together on alert cycles and flying, Troy and Wendy wanted to get to know more about them and their families. They planned a barbecue for the next Saturday afternoon.

Joe Mangino, Troy's new bomb-nav, and his wife, Gail, had been married almost a year. She was a gregarious, blue-eyed blonde and a graduate of Stanford's School of Journalism. She met Joe while doing a story on March AFB for the *Los Angeles Times*. Mangino had a degree in civil engineering from the University of Arizona, where he had been on a football scholarship until he blew out his knee during his sophomore year. Needing money to finish college, he joined the Air Force ROTC.

Bill Candee, Troy's new copilot, was born and raised on a ranch outside of Lubbock. He was a freespirited Texan who walked with a swagger and peppered his speech with Texas witticisms and sordid language. He had played four years of football for the Red Raiders of Texas Tech and had a degree in animal husbandry. His girlfriend, Beth McDonald, was a cute blonde who taught fifth grade in the Riverside school system.

Annabelle DeLuca and Mark Denman rounded out the guest list. Annabelle had moved back to California after finishing her degree at ASU, and the relationship between the two had blossomed.

On the day of the barbecue, the women moved

inside to chat and prepare the food that went with the steaks Troy was grilling. Outside, the men watched the barbecue coals heat up, gulped down Budweisers, and talked flying.

"Colonel Blauw gave me a heads-up the other day," Troy said. "Have you guys sensed any animosity, or have you heard any negative comments about my quick upgrade to aircraft commander?"

"You know, Troy," Joe Mangino said with a shrug, "there'll be some who are jealous of your early upgrade, particularly since you're an Academy puke, but they're the people who are always whining about something. We're going to be a damn fine crew, and I wouldn't worry about it. I for one am happy to be flying with you. After all, you and I have a special bond—we shared Diablo together. I sure as hell feel safe flying with you." Joe raised his beer high in a silent mock salute.

"Hell, Troy," Bill Candee said, "I wouldn't give a crap about those jealous bastards, if there are any. They're usually the folks at the bottom of the totem pole who haven't a clue about how to get to the top. Screw 'em. We've got more important stuff to do. We're gonna be the best."

Mark Denman chimed in with his support. "You know what? This world is full of assholes, but their kind usually doesn't draw much of an audience. What I heard last week while I was on alert, mostly from copilots, was that they want you guys to succeed. Everyone is pretty proud of what you did that night, Troy. I personally haven't heard anyone question your right to a crew. They're rooting for you; they want you to do well. They figure if *you're* successful, it'll alert the brass to the fact that the rest of us young pilots don't have to have a couple thousand hours before we're upgraded to aircraft commanders. Another thing, while I'm thinking of it—thank you for putting in a good word with Colonel Kurfman for me to replace you on his crew. We had a long talk yesterday, and it looks like I'm his new copilot, thanks to you."

"That's a good break for you, Mark," Troy said. "I'm glad you're with him. You'll get some good stick time since he's an IP."

"Yeah, dammit, I'm jealous," Bill said.

Troy raised his beer and addressed his new crew members. "Thanks, guys, for your candidness. Let's go for the roses."

"Hey, you good-lookin' studs! Are the steaks ready yet, or have you burned them to death?" Wendy called as the women filed out of the back door, loaded down with silverware, plates and napkins and all of the fixings for a grand California barbecue.

....

The next few weeks were packed tight with hard work. SAC Reg. 51-19 set high standards for upgrading to combat-ready status. Troy flew his first instructional flight with Colonel Kurfman. He found it strange to be in the front aircraft commander's seat with Kurfman in the backseat. Troy really enjoyed flying with Kurfman, but since he had been Kurfman's copilot, the staff thought it more professional that Troy fly the remainder of his check flights with other squadron IPs.

He had some trouble at first with night refueling, and landing from the front seat took some getting used to, but it wasn't long before he became comfortable with both. After six training flights, the squadron thought the crew was ready for their standardization evaluation, or stand-eval, check ride. The check mission included a nighttime heavyweight refueling, two RBS bomb runs, two nighttime celestial navigation legs, and a nighttime low-level into Diablo.

During the mission, Troy felt a little spooky calling Albuquerque Center to request permission to enter Diablo. Before he could wonder whether they would remember him, they asked if this was the same Disco Three-eight that had visited them a few months earlier. Troy thanked them for their assistance that memorable night, and they acknowledged that they had been relieved to hear that everything turned out well.

After several weeks of intense training, the crew passed their final check flight and became a fully qualified, SAC combat-ready bomber crew with the designation of E-38. The following week Troy received a note in the mail with the return address of "Commander-in-Chief, SAC." He ripped it open. Written in longhand was the following message:

Congratulations on becoming combat-ready. I know you'll be a fine aircraft commander.

Robert A. Strong, General, USAF

Chapter IX

THE WING FOUND FRESH blood in Troy's new, combat-ready crew; they pulled seventy-two-hour alert duty, six weekends in a row.

The hardened underground alert facility at March AFB was equipped with reading rooms, a mess-facility open sixteen hours a day, and a rec room with pool and Ping-Pong tables. Outside the facility was a family-friendly area with horseshoe pits, volleyball and handball courts, barbecues, and a children's play area. In the evenings and on weekends, it substituted as a gathering place for crews and their families. These get-togethers relieved the stress and fatigue of mothers stuck at home over long periods with small children. They also lowered tensions resulting from crew members living together in tight quarters for seventy-two plus hours at a time. Klaxon horns, installed base-wide, allowed a third of the crews to be away from the alert facility for short trips to the base exchange or the club.

Sometimes Wendy picked up Gail and Beth and drove to the base, fortified with all the fixings for an outdoor picnic. Often the piercing sounds of the alert klaxon interrupted their gatherings. Crews dropped whatever they were doing and scrambled into their alert vehicles, blue emergency lights flashing as they sped to the flightline and to their nuclear-weapon-carrying B-47s. The bombers were configured in a cocked position; by flipping a half dozen switches, the engines and the plane's electronic gear roared to life. Bombers taxied within five minutes of the first sounds of the klaxon.

....

Three-week deployments, code named REFLEX, positioned SAC's nuclear-carrying bombers and aircrews at forward overseas bases where they could strike Soviet targets within three to five hours after takeoff—without the hassle and delay of airborne refueling. The wing at March normally deployed to Pacific bases: Guam or Eielson Air Force Base in Alaska. But due to heightened Cold War tensions—the Soviets had placed medium-range ballistic missiles in Cuba—SAC chose to reinforce its nuclear strike force at forward bases in Britain and Spain. The wing's staging base in the UK was Brize Norton, a British Royal Air Force base eighty miles west of London.

Troy's crew was scheduled to deploy in mid-October. He looked forward to the experience, although he hated leaving Wendy.

....

As Troy released the brakes on Disco Three-eight, it began picking up speed as it rolled down the centerline of the two-mile-long March AFB runway. It was 5:20 the evening of October 18. Destination: the UK. The mission was the first big test for Troy's new crew, with Joe Mangino up front and Bill Candee in the co-pilot's seat. Troy also had a crew chief stuffed in the fourth-man position, which gave him added comfort if for any reason he had to land at a strange base. The crew completed three polar celestial navigation legs and two nighttime airborne refuelings, flying a great-circle route across the frozen Canadian Hudson Bay and over the white icecaps of Greenland. They ended the long mission with a simulated bomb run on the outskirts of London.

They landed at Brize the following morning, almost twelve hours after takeoff. It was a tough, physically exhausting mission, but Troy felt good about his new crew's accomplishment. They had worked together well during the long flight. Troy was especially excited about having successfully completed two nighttime airborne refueling hookups—a major accomplishment and confidence builder.

After barely twenty-four hours of crew rest, Troy

and his crew briefed the alert force commander on their assigned war-plan target: a Soviet airbase thirty miles north of Moscow. Following extensive questioning, the commander certified Disco Three-eight for alert duty. Proceeding to the flight line, the crew checked the aircraft and accepted and signed for the 3.2-megaton nuclear weapon lashed securely in their bomb bay.

A specialized briefing in the evening updated the crews on the volatile Cuban missile crisis. On October 22, they listened to President Kennedy address the nation. For the first time, the president publicly acknowledged that the Soviets had placed nuclear-tipped, medium-range ballistic missiles on Cuban soil. With a range of twelve hundred miles, these missiles threatened every town in the eastern third of the United States. The president also announced the start of a naval blockade surrounding Cuba.

On Wednesday morning, October 24—the deadline for the blockade—two Soviet freighters drew near the quarantine line five hundred miles east of Cuba. The Pentagon went to Defcon 2 (defense condition)—Defcon 5 is peace; Defcon 1 is war—sending out the order in the clear so there could be no misunderstanding by the Soviets. All fourteen hundred SAC B-47 and B-52 nuclear-carrying bombers went on a heightened, around-the-clock combat alert.

The Brize Norton alert force commander, Lieutenant Colonel Hobson, called the crews to the briefing room at 3:00 AM. They were informed that an American U-2 high-altitude spy plane had been shot down over Cuba and its Air Force pilot, Major Rudolph Anderson, killed. The mood in the briefing room was somber. Troy and his crew thought they may surely be going to war.

Troy's primary target was a sprawling Soviet airbase north of Moscow that housed intercontinental missiles, two squadrons of MiG-17s and SU-9 (Fishpot) high-altitude fighters, and a detachment of multi-engine Bison bombers. Intelligence also suspected that the area might be defended by SA-2 surface-to-air missiles. It was a good target that the crew could hit four hours after takeoff and without airborne refueling. Troy was confident that they could get in and destroy the target—maybe with enough fuel to recover back to England. If they couldn't make it back, they would look for a suitable poststrike NATO landing field in Denmark or West Germany. Troy and crew spent the morning studying intelligence reports on the target areas.

On the way out the door, the squadron intelligence officer asked each crew member to review his personnel data and check his E&E (escape and evasion) personal authenticator. The SAR (search and rescue) forces used the authenticators to confirm the identities of downed airmen in enemy territory before initiating a rescue. Troy's authenticator was "The name of my first dog was Blackie." Candee and Mangino also used the names of their first dogs.

Fourteen B-47s were parked in echelon at forty-five degrees on the parking aprons and taxi strips at Brize Norton. Troy was parked in number three position. Power carts, operating around the clock, kept electrical power on the aircraft. The crews ran checks on the nuclear weapon's electrical circuitry twice a day. With the alert bombers in this "hot" configuration, all it took for the engines to roar to life was the tripping of a few switches. The first airplane would be off the ground in three minutes or less. With around-the-clock manning, the cold and uncomfortably cramped airplane cockpits took on a distinctive aura of their own. To help relieve the stress, crews were rotated — two hours on, two hours off.

On October 27, later referred to as Black Saturday, it appeared that negotiations between Washington and Moscow had worsened. SAC was ordered to go to a modified Defcon 1 that required 10 percent of the alert force crews to be in their seats with engines running. This ensured that SAC would get at least 10 percent of its nuke strike force off the ground before Soviet intercontinental missiles could destroy runways. The fact that SAC had gone to this highly lethal launch status was purposely leaked to journalists so that the Soviets would be aware of it. The risk of escalation through a miscalculation was high—and growing.

At the same time, a cat-and-mouse game had been unfolding in Washington. At 8:00 PM, the White House publicly broadcast the president's letter to Khrushchev, pledging not to invade Cuba if Khrushchev removed all missiles from Cuban soil. It called for a response no later than 4:00 PM the next day, Sunday.

After thirty-six hours of sitting, off and on, in a cold and increasingly foul-smelling cockpit with only short catnaps to bolster energy, Troy could sense that tensions were running high. Everyone's physical and mental stamina was beginning to wane.

Back-and-forth cockpit chatter increased as the hours slowly churned on. Troy was aware of the increased tension and the effect it was having on his crew. Mangino had reviewed his charts into and out of the target area so many times that he had memorized more than twenty names of small Soviet villages, from Kalipeda on the Baltic Sea to Klin near the target area. Each of the crew members had taken turns at trying to pronounce the names. Troy encouraged these mental diversions.

As it became painfully apparent that the crisis might not get resolved peacefully, and that World War III might indeed be near at hand, the interphone conversations between the crew members took on a more serious turn.

Responding to a question, Mangino said, "Ya know, guys, I don't have a problem arming that nuke in our bomb bay. I'm also okay with flipping that red-guarded 'pickle' switch that mechanically ensures release of the bomb, because it's not me who's making the call to drop it. The president's making that decision, hopefully after listening to a whole bunch of smart people. My job's the easy one. The only thing I have to do is make darn sure the nuke works right and that it hits the ground where it's supposed to. I pray we don't have to drop it. And I pray that some cool heads on both sides prevail and that this thing gets resolved quickly and peacefully."

"I'm all for that," Candee said over the interphone. "SAC's taken just about every human aspect out of our hands. Their positive control system, with its built-in safeguards, pretty well eliminates any screw-ups by us. With each of us having to independently decode and authenticate a launch order, and then all of us having to agree before we can even *think* about dropping the thing, it's about as fail-safe as the human condition permits."

"Yeah," Troy agreed. "We're simply the final mechanism to carry out the president's wishes—his mechanical arm of execution, so to speak."

"I wonder if the folks back home have any idea how close we are right now to World War III?" Mangino asked.

"I doubt it," Troy said. "I'll bet they're going about their normal Saturday activities—washing their car, talking to the neighbors. And you know what? Maybe it's best that way."

Candee keyed his mike switch. "Just thought of something: we just might be safer here in a war zone than the folks are back home. They could very likely be the recipients of a retaliatory nuclear holocaust from Soviet missiles. Hell, the only thing *we've* got to worry about is getting shot down. Maybe we'd better say a prayer for the folks back home? If I were a betting man, I'd say there's about a 90/10 probability we're going to launch. And as an old Catholic altar boy from West Texas, I've been praying that if we do drop that baby, we do it with finite accuracy and then get the hell out of Dodge."

"Amen to that," Troy replied. His thoughts turned to his family members as silence settled over the aircraft. After a moment, Candee broke the quiet with a groan.

"Are your butts as sore as mine?" asked Candee. "Man, sitting on this survival pack for hours is harder than being glued to a saddle, riding fence all day. Ya almost wish something would happen. This is boring as hell!"

"Be careful what you ask for, Bill," Troy warned.

"I wonder whether the B-29 crew that dropped the

big one on Hiroshima had the same thoughts we're having," Mangino commented.

"Probably," Troy said. "Hey, by the way, did you hear what happened on Captain Bob Brodski's crew yesterday? Bob had been assigned a new copilot, a lieutenant fresh out of pilot training. Believe his name was Callahan. Brodski thought the guy was acting a little strange and a bit pensive after they'd finished briefing the alert force commander on their target, but he wrote it off as just due to his personality and first-time jitters.

"But yesterday, after they preflighted their airplane and accepted the weapon, they were sitting in the cockpit discussing route and target info. Callahan abruptly told Brodski over the interphone that he'd arrived at a decision based on his religious faith—and that his faith didn't allow him to be involved in dropping a nuclear weapon that could kill thousands of people. Whereupon, he unbuckled from his copilot seat and started to climb down the ladder and out of the airplane."

"Christ, what did Brodski do?" asked Candee.

"Well, you know Brodski's a combat vet with over seventy B-26 missions in Korea. He promptly unsnapped his .45 automatic from its shoulder holster and pointed it at Callahan's forehead. He shouted, 'You take one more damn step down that ladder,

Lieutenant, and you're a dead man. Get your ass back in that copilot seat … *now.*'

"From what I'm told, Callahan hesitated for about a half a second, and then climbed back into the seat."

"Wow! My kind of guy. Always did like Bob Brodski," Candee said with a chuckle. "Do you think Brodski would've shot Callahan if he'd kept going?"

"Guess we'll never know," Troy said. "Have to assume Callahan wasn't sure either. He was ordered back to March—left on a tanker this morning. He'll face some disciplinary action. Probably end up flying a trash hauler."

"Hey, Troy, what *about* Callahan's religious faith?" Joe asked. "Does he have a legal argument?"

Troy's response was swift. "You know when we put on this uniform and take the oath, some things change. That doesn't mean we compromise our religious faith—or nonfaith, for that matter. But when we put on the uniform, the cause is not ours to decide; it becomes ours to defend."

Troy was interrupted by a shout from the ramp below. "Hey, Bench! You guys awake up there?"

"Sounds like our relief crew has arrived," Troy said. "Joe, before you leave, make sure you get the new crew to sign for the weapon. I'm heading into OPS for an intel update."

....

To everyone's surprise, on Sunday afternoon the

Soviets agreed to dismantle and withdraw their missiles from Cuba. Khrushchev stated, "In order to save the world, we must retreat." Reason prevailed, and the crisis ended abruptly. America had gone eyeball to eyeball with the Soviets, and the Soviets blinked first.

It was Troy's first "almost-taste" of combat. He was proud of his crew. They had worked as a team through some very stressful and tiring hours. Troy felt that they had been prepared physically and psychologically to launch and strike their Soviet target if ordered to do so. Having been tested, the entire SAC bomber force had proved it was up to the task.

....

Troy had tried for several days to get a call through to Wendy. He finally connected. "Hi, darling. God, it's good to hear your voice."

"Oh, honey, I'm so happy to hear from you. I know you guys have been really busy, but I was so worried about you. I tried calling, but I wasn't able to get through. How are you doing now?"

"I'm fine, sweetie. We should be home in about a week. I can't wait to see you." Troy glanced back at the long line of crew members waiting to use the phone. "Honey, I'm sorry this is short, but I have to get off the line. I love you so much, and I really miss you."

"I miss you, too, Troy. I love you, my darling. Bye."

Chapter X

Other than bucking a two-hundred-mile-per-hour jet stream most of the way, the return flight from Brize Norton to March was uneventful. After a lengthy debriefing, Troy was handed a note to report to Lieutenant Colonel Blauw's office at eight o'clock the following morning.

When he knocked on the commander's half-open door, Blauw was on the phone but motioned for him to come in and take a seat. Blauw's first words when he got off the phone were, "You're out of uniform, Bench." Troy, wearing a clean flying suit, was confused by the comment. He thought, *this is so out of character for the colonel.*

"Dammit, what's the matter with you young guys? You can't keep track of the proper uniform insignia?" A broad smile then appeared on Blauw's face as he reached across his desk and unfolded his clenched hand. In his open palm was a pair of silver captain bars.

"Congratulations, Captain, you got promoted two years early. And Troy," he added, "you earned it the hard way."

Troy was flabbergasted. As he tried to regain his composure, he searched for the words to express his surprise and humility. Finally, he blurted out, "Thank you, Colonel. I don't know what to say. Sir, thank you for all of your support and confidence in me."

....

Troy put the red Corvette in high gear and raced home. He and Wendy celebrated that evening by dining at the elegant Mission Inn in Riverside.

When he ordered martinis, Wendy interrupted, "I'll just have a Coke."

"Are you feeling okay?" Troy asked with concern, but she assured him that she was fine.

When the waiter departed, Wendy reached across the table, clasped his hands, and with an angelic smile like none Troy had ever seen, she exclaimed, "Darling, we're going to be parents!"

"Oh my God … Oh my God …" As hard as he tried, he couldn't find words for the occasion. Finally, he stammered, "Honey, my darling, I'm just so happy. Wow! God has truly blessed us with His magic wand today."

....

Having returned from overseas alert duty, Troy was given the standard five working days off plus the adjoining weekends. He and Wendy decided to use the time to drive to Santa Barbara and spend a few leisurely days at the luxurious Biltmore Hotel on the Pacific coastline.

On the way to Santa Barbara, Troy's mind had raced from one subject to another. Something was troubling him, but he hadn't been able to nail it down—getting a crew, being promoted, finding out they had a baby on the way ... maybe it was a combination of all of them. Or could it have been the letter from IBM that was waiting for him upon his return from England?

Stewart Brown III, a vice president at IBM, had seen Troy on television during his media tour a few months earlier. In his letter, Brown congratulated Troy for courageously landing his crippled bomber. Brown wrote that he had been an Air Force pilot in Korea and wanted to talk with Troy about a job with IBM.

Troy hadn't mentioned any of this to Wendy; he didn't want to trouble her until he had organized his own thoughts. But she had guessed something was up, and in her inimitable way, pinned him down as they drove to Santa Barbara.

"Okay, Captain, let's talk about what's troubling you," she announced. "Is it the way I dress? The way

I burn your toast in the morning? Or could it be my imperfect housecleaning? Out with it, Mr. Bench."

They laughed, but then Wendy turned serious. "Look, hon, I know you got this job offer from Mr. Big Shot at IBM. You know I'm a mind reader and I can see through envelopes. With all that's going on in your life now, could it be that you're questioning whether you want to stay in the Air Force?"

The thought of getting out of the Air Force had never consciously crossed Troy's mind before. After all, he was an Air Force Academy grad.

Wendy continued. "Or could it be that close brush with an all-out nuclear exchange that you just went through? Maybe you're questioning your resolve to drop a bomb that could snuff out thousands of lives. Darling, if you want to discuss any of this stuff, let me know. I promise to be a good sounding board."

Troy was a little annoyed that Wendy could read his mind so well.

"Thanks, hon. I'll let you know."

The next morning Troy was up early. He took a five-mile jog along the beach, and then jumped into the ocean for a swim to clear his head.

From their hotel balcony, Wendy could see him stretched out on the beach. She donned a swimsuit, grabbed some coffee and bagels, and walked down to join him.

After finishing their continental breakfast, Wendy

sprinted toward the ocean for a swim. Troy's eyes followed her until she disappeared into the surf. *My God, what a beautiful woman,* he thought. *I've got to be the luckiest guy on Earth. This gorgeous, talented, sensitive, and understanding woman loves me with all her heart and is bearing my child. How could I possibly be troubled about anything? All I have to do is love her back and make her happy.*

When Wendy returned from her swim, Troy had dozed off on the warm sand. Waking him with a gentle kiss on his forehead, she insisted that they talk about whatever was troubling him.

"First, I want to know what you were thinking when you were sitting in your bomber at Brize Norton, knowing that at any moment you could be headed toward your target and dropping a bomb that might kill thousands. I know you had classes on this morality stuff at the Academy. Will you tell me your feelings on it?"

Troy's mind raced back to his Catholic upbringing and the teachings of the fourth-century teacher/philosopher, Saint Augustine. "You know, when I was a teenager in Bisbee I memorized Saint Augustine's precepts on war. I still remember them." Troy looked skyward as if the early morning clouds would suddenly enlighten him about Saint Augustine. "First, war must have the authority of the sovereign—not just an individual. Second, war has to be for a just cause, not for vengeance. And finally, war should be based on rightful intentions, the advancement of good over evil."

"That's fine, Troy, but can you live with those precepts now? More importantly, could you drop a bomb or *not* drop a bomb based on those precepts?"

"Yes, I *do* believe they're good guidelines. When I was at the Academy I took a philosophy course that dealt with war and morality in the military profession, and it basically reinforced those same principles. I feel secure in my belief that a sovereign nation should be able to defend itself, as well as protect the weak and the innocent from unjust attack and oppression. That's one of the reasons I went to the Academy, and it's one of the reasons I love the military—it's part of what we do."

"Well then, how about dropping a nuclear bomb that can kill thousands? Can you do that?"

"I have no problem with dropping a nuke when the president authorizes it. I'm at peace with myself in that regard."

"Okay, Mr. Bench, that leaves just one unresolved question: are you sure you want to spend the next twenty or thirty years in the Air Force, or do you want to go out into the corporate world and make lots of money?"

"That's one thing I love about you, Wendy. You go right to the heart of an issue," Troy said with an affectionate chuckle. "God … I've never considered leaving the Air Force. It's always been my intention to make the military my career … but now, with a baby on the way, I keep thinking about being away from you and my family for long periods, and the hassle it will be for us to move all the time. I owe it to you and our unborn to keep an open mind on this IBM offer."

"Honey, that's all I want you to do. Just keep an open mind, so when you arrive at that final decision you'll be satisfied that you've looked at everything," Wendy said reassuringly. "And, sweetheart, you know I'll be happy as a military wife—and I could be just as happy being the wife of a rich corporate executive. I'll be okay with whatever you decide, Troy."

Snuggling her damp upper body tightly into his chest, Wendy stretched up and kissed him. "I love you, Troy."

Later that day, Troy got on the phone and scheduled a meeting with Stewart Brown III, vice president for engineering and research at IBM's downtown Los Angeles offices. Brown extended an invitation for Wendy to join them.

Mr. Brown and his wife were waiting in his well-appointed office on Wilshire Boulevard. "Troy, please call me Stewart. I'd like you to meet my wife, Betty."

After the introductions, the women departed on a prearranged shopping trip on Rodeo Drive. For the first half hour or so, Stewart and Troy discussed flying and the new jet-age Air Force. Troy felt comfortable and at ease with him.

Stewart had flown forty-six combat missions in B-26s in Korea in 1950, but he had never flown jets. Upon returning to civilian life, Stewart had completed his engineering degree at Stanford and jumped on board with IBM during its early expansion, rising to vice president in just ten years.

"Troy, please understand that I'm not trying to proselytize you away from the Air Force. I feel very strongly about keeping good people in our armed forces. As far as I'm concerned, there's no American institution that comes close to equaling our military services for building character and honesty and instilling a value for hard work in young men and women.

"But while watching you on national TV several months ago, I was impressed with the way you handled yourself. So, today I want to talk with you about IBM and what a future in this company could mean for you and your family. Then you make the call, Troy. It's your decision."

Following a quick tour of the facility, Stewart introduced Troy to two other vice presidents. Troy soon realized he *was* being proselytized, but he had to admit it felt good. They later joined Wendy and Betty for a late lunch at the world-famous Ciro's restaurant. As they parted, Stewart told Troy that he would receive a letter from IBM within a week.

"Wow, what a day!" Troy exclaimed as he and Wendy drove back to Santa Barbara to finish their short vacation. They talked excitedly about what had transpired. Upon their return to Riverside two days later, they found an IBM letter waiting in the mailbox. Troy and Wendy sat together and read it.

"Betty and I so much enjoyed meeting you and Wendy," the letter began. Stewart went on to outline how Troy's background would fit into the rapidly expanding IBM family. The bottom line was a job offer in engineering research that paid four times what Troy was making in the Air Force, plus an offer of an advanced degree at the company's expense. Troy and Wendy were stunned; they had never expected anything close to that kind of offer. How in the world could he turn it down—a stable job in a well-respected, futuristic company with fantastic pay and education benefits? Their minds whirled with excitement.

The electricity of the moment, however, was interrupted by a phone call from Lieutenant Colonel Blauw. "Troy, you and your crew are to be at base ops, in Class A uniform, at eight o'clock Monday morning. Your crew has been requested by name. A KC-135 tanker will transport you to SAC headquarters at Omaha."

"Sir, can you tell me what this is about?"

"I have no idea, Troy, but I'd suggest you pack for a weeklong stay. Good luck."

Chapter XI

DEPLANING ON A DAMP, foggy morning at Offutt AFB near Omaha, Troy and his crew were met by a young lieutenant in a well-starched khaki uniform.

"My name is Roger Danforth, and I'll be your escort while you're here," the lieutenant said, extending his hand to greet each crewmember.

Settling into a blue Air Force staff car with their luggage, Troy asked Danforth if he knew *why* they were at Offutt and how long they would be there. But his questions went unanswered as Danforth silently drove them to a double fenced compound at an isolated part of the base. A heavily armed security guard at the gate checked their IDs against copies of orders that noted their top secret security clearances.

Once inside, Danforth ushered the crew from one secure underground area to another. Troy sensed they were burrowing deeper into the bowels of a solid concrete compound. At each checkpoint their IDs and orders were rechecked against an access list bearing their names.

Guided down a brightly lit corridor adorned with framed colorful sketches of futuristic Air Force weaponry, Danforth led Troy and his crew into a small, windowless theater.

"Captain Bench, I'll be leaving you here," Danforth said. "You'll be receiving a briefing in this room very shortly. I'll make sure your bags are dropped off in your rooms at the BOQ."

Reaching into his pocket, Danforth pulled out a card with his phone number and handed it to Troy. "If you need anything, sir, give me a call." Troy thanked him, and the crew took seats in the front row of the sparsely filled theater.

As he sat waiting, Troy detected a faint, musty odor that reminded him of the iron oxide smell in the underground mines of Bisbee. Based on their lengthy walk he guessed they must be at least fifty feet below ground level. Glancing around the room, he counted eight other crews whose members appeared to be about the same ranks as his crew—lieutenants and captains. The crews talked among themselves in hushed tones in the dimly lit theater. Mangino leaned toward Troy and whispered, "What the hell have we gotten ourselves into, boss?" Troy shrugged. They didn't have to wait long to find out.

A tall, slim colonel with ruddy features, high cheek

bones, and the outward appearance of a marathon athlete entered the room gripping a large coffee mug that bore the colorful Strategic Air Command shield. The crews came to attention.

"Gentlemen, take your seats," he said. "I'm Colonel Jack Sparks, deputy assistant director for plans and programs here at SAC headquarters." Glancing to his left and motioning with his hand, "with me is Lieutenant Colonel Stan Zuko from the Directorate of Intelligence. I know you gentlemen are anxious to find out why you're here, so let's get started."

With that, Sparks motioned to the projectionist at the rear of the room. "Okay, Sergeant, roll the tape."

The eight-minute black-and-white sixteen millimeter movie depicted B-47s in high-speed, low-level, overwater maneuvers terminating with max-climb and steep-turn tactics in what appeared to be simulated bomb runs. Other shots illuminated the tense facial expressions of crewmembers as they executed the maneuvers under very turbulent conditions. A series of exterior shots focused on the flexing of the B-47 wings as heavy buffeting made them quiver like the thin steel blade of a carpenter's hand saw. A notation on the movie indicated that the maneuvers had been performed at Eglin AFB by the Boeing Company.

Recalling his Air Force Academy classes in aerospace engineering, Troy tried to imagine the structural impact on the bomber's wing components during the abrupt maneuvers. A sickening feeling erupted in the pit of his stomach, a sense of anxiety he hadn't experienced since his first week at the Academy. He had a sensation that he and his crew were about to become guinea pigs for something big, but he couldn't connect the dots. He wondered why a representative from the intelligence community was sitting in on the briefing. His thoughts were interrupted as the movie ended and the lights in the room brightened.

Colonel Sparks strode back to the podium. "Gentlemen, you're going to be performing those maneuvers flawlessly within a few short weeks." Gasps and mumbled whispering could be heard throughout the theater. Sparks continued, "To learn these high-speed, max-performance tactics you'll be placed on temporary duty orders to Eglin AFB. Your training there will last about three weeks. Upon your departure from Eglin, you'll receive new TDY orders directing you to a forward base for a period of up to three months. I apologize that I'm not at liberty to provide you with additional information."

Troy searched the colonel's face for some hint of an explanation but found none. Sparks continued, "I *can* tell you this much—the training program and subsequent TDY won't be a cakewalk. It's going to be a tough, demanding flying program. I also want to make very clear that this program is voluntary. Tomorrow you'll be given an opportunity to back out. If you choose that route, there'll be no prejudice incurred and no reference to it on your records. Are there any questions?"

After a few seconds of silence, Troy stood up. "Sir, I'm Captain Troy Bench from the 22nd Bomb Wing at March Air Force Base. As I look around the room, all I see are young crews. I imagine that most of us have no more than a thousand to fifteen hundred flying hours. I would think that SAC would want their most experienced crews to be involved in high-performance flying such as this, not relatively young crews with few flying hours like us. Can you explain why SAC picked crews with our experience level?"

"Good question, Bench, but I can't discuss that with you now." With that dismissal, Sparks abruptly ended the questioning. "Okay, if there are no more questions, a bus will pick you up in front of the building and take you to the BOQ. Tomorrow morning a bus will be waiting in front of the club at 7:00 AM to bring you back to this building. At that time, I'll have a volunteer mission statement for you to sign. All crewmembers must sign the statement or the entire crew becomes ineligible for this operation. Those who volunteer will be here in class for the next two days; those who choose otherwise will return to their respective bases.

"I must emphasize that you are not to discuss this information with anyone who is not presently in this room—not with your wives, girlfriends, or anyone at your base, including your commanders. Tomorrow everyone will sign a statement to that effect. To assist you in that regard, you'll be provided a cover story. I caution you not to theorize about this operation, because you'll undoubtedly be wrong. Gentlemen, you're excused. I'll see you all here in the morning."

No one spoke as the crews exited the theater, led by a security guard, and made their way up the lengthy corridor to ground level and the reception area. While waiting for the bus to arrive, Troy stepped outside to clear his head. Gazing at the endless flat, green landscape of Offutt, he wondered how an airbase came to be built in the middle of this Midwest farm belt. A bronze plaque, denoting some history embedded on a decorative fountain, provided part of the answer.

Troy learned that Offutt dated back to the late nineteenth century when it was a frontier Army outpost. Some of the original red brick buildings covered by layers of thick, green ivy reminded a visitor of the base's historic past. During the early part of the twentieth century, the fort became home to an Army aviation unit, and in 1948, because of its central location, Offutt became headquarters for the newly formed Strategic Air Command.

Following late afternoon naps, Troy and his crew walked across the street to the Officers' Club. Selecting a table in an isolated corner of the bar, they sat down to discuss their new mission.

"Okay, here's the deal," Troy said between sips of his beer. "We're going to make this decision as a crew. I want to hear your candid views after I give a few of my own. First of all, I'm confident we wouldn't be here if we weren't a well-respected crew—our names weren't just plucked out of a hat. I'm also convinced this has to be a damn important program for SAC."

Leaning in closer to the table, Troy shifted his eye contact from one crewmember to the other and spoke slowly. "There's no question the flying is going to be hairy. At this point the only thing we know for sure is that we're going to be flying a jet bomber, an airplane designed to fly at high altitude and at normal jet speeds, at high speed and at max-performance. I want to make it clear I believe we are going to be involved in some dangerous flying. Colonel Sparks told us that it wasn't going to be a cakewalk, and I take him at his word."

Troy shifted in his seat and donned somewhat of a puzzled look. "One thing I haven't figured out is why the lieutenant colonel from intel was at the briefing. It's possible this thing could turn out to have a clandestine twist. But now I'm theorizing and Colonel Sparks cautioned us against that. Another thing I don't understand is the reasoning behind the use of younger crews. And finally, guys, if we choose to volunteer, I can almost guarantee you that the next few months are going to be exciting as hell. Okay, with that off my mind, now it's your turn. Joe you go first."

Mangino leaned forward, resting his muscular forearms on the table's edge. With a meditative look, he lowered his eyes and spoke slowly. "Ah, well, I have to confess that Gail and I have always discussed things like this together, and over time, we've usually come to an agreement—"

"Good Lord, man," Candee interrupted, "that must be the reason I never got married. For God's sake, Joe, do you married guys all have to consult with your wives?"

Troy annoyed at the interruption, looked sternly at Candee and said, "I'll answer that. Yeah, Candee, most married people do just that, particularly if they want to stay married." Turning back toward Mangino, who seemed to have ignored Candee's comment, Troy added, "Now go ahead, Joe. Finish your thoughts."

"Well, anyway, this afternoon I called Gail and told her something had come up that may take me away for a few months. You know what she said? She said, 'Joe, I've got my part-time job at the *Los Angeles Times* that'll keep me busy. So if you're sure you want to do this, I'm okay with it; it's your call, Joe.' God, I'm lucky to have a wife like her."

"Oh, for Christ's sake, Joe, stop it. You're gonna make me puke," Bill snorted.

Without acknowledging the interruption, Joe continued, "Guys, I have confidence that SAC knows what they're doing. Besides, whatever it is, it's got to be exciting and, I'm convinced, worthwhile. We're a damn fine crew. I know we'll stick together and take care of each other when the chips are down. And regardless of how it turns out, I'm confident we'll be okay and that we'll all come through it together. I'm bettin' on it. So, count me in."

Reaching across the table, Troy gave Joe a reassuring pat on the arm.

"Okay, Bill, let's hear your thoughts." Troy said, looking at his copilot.

"You know what? I'm free as hell. I've got no wife, although Beth sometimes tries to act like one. I've got nothing to lose. Hell, I was brought up on a West Texas ranch roping steers and breaking broncos. What can be more dangerous than that? Anyway, I was getting bored hanging out with you guys on alert. Excitement was part of the reason I joined the Air Force. I like a little danger occasionally, and I love excitement. And who knows, when we finish this little thing, SAC may just be so indebted to me, they'll offer me my own crew. So, gents, I say, let's do it."

Troy stared directly at his bomb-nav and copilot and took a deep breath. "As I said before, there's a whole lot more to this thing than we know. I can't tell you why, but I have a distinct feeling that this is going to be a major event in our lives, and it's not going to be for the fainthearted. There's a sizable danger factor involved here that we ought not overlook. They wouldn't be asking us to sign a volunteer statement if it were simply a run-of-the-mill flying exercise."

Moving closer, and with a more serious look on his face, Troy made eye contact with both Joe and Bill and spoke slowly but firmly. "Okay, I'm making a promise to you guys here and now. I'll do my level best to ensure that we all come through this thing in one piece. This I *promise* you."

His lips spread in a slow smile. "Well, guys, it looks to me like we've got a crew decision. Let's toast to this new venture."

Three glass mugs clanked in midair, setting the wheels in motion for a grand new adventure.

....

The following morning the crews met with Colonel Sparks. Eight signed volunteer statements; the ninth couldn't convince the copilot, whose wife was pregnant, to volunteer. The remaining eight were given orders for Eglin AFB, Florida, stating that:

"You will participate in a flight test program involving over-water tactics for a period not to exceed thirty days. The program will be referred to by its unclassified code name, Shark Bite, with an aircraft callsign of Shark."

"That is your cover story," Colonel Sparks said. "And that's all you need to know for now."

Troy and crew had a hard time staying awake during the next two days of boring ground school. They familiarized themselves with revised aircraft performance data and learned to operate new pieces of electronic equipment installed on the B-47s they would fly at Eglin. During that time, Sparks gave no indication of what was to take place in the follow-on TDY to a forward base. "You will be told in due time," he promised.

On the third day the crews returned to their home bases with orders to report to Eglin in five days.

....

Wendy had just stepped out of the shower as Troy opened the door to their small Riverside apartment. Throwing on her white terrycloth robe, she rushed toward him, flinging her arms around him and holding him so tightly he could barely breathe. Her skin exuded the intoxicating smell of her perfumed soap, a smell that Troy loved. As her robe fell open to expose her partially wet body, Troy scooped her up into his arms. They kissed deeply as he whisked her into the bedroom to make passionate love. Later, relaxing in each other's arms, Wendy spoke softly, "Troy, I'm so glad you're home. I've missed you terribly."

"Darling, you can't guess how happy I am to be here." Troy whispered back.

The next few days were like a second honey-moon—or at least they were until Troy dropped the bomb.

"I could be gone for the next several months," he told her carefully. "We're testing some new tactics for SAC at Eglin Air Force Base in Florida. I have no idea why we were selected but I'm sure SAC had a good reason."

Troy hated seeing Wendy cry. She'd always been the good-trooper Air Force wife, so he attributed it to the emotional highs and lows of being pregnant.

The next day, Troy sorted through a pile of un-opened mail. An envelope with a colorful IBM logo caught his eye, and he quickly tore it open. It was a personal letter from Stewart Brown. In the first couple of paragraphs Stewart wrote how impressed he had been with Troy's accomplishments, and how he and his wife had enjoyed meeting Wendy. Stewart closed the letter by stating, "Troy, I hope you have given posi-tive consideration to our offer and will soon be joining our IBM family."

Wendy detected uncertainty in Troy's demeanor as he stared blankly into space, slowly stroking the letter and not knowing quite what to do about it.

In a comforting voice she asked, "Honey, have you decided what you want to do yet? You know you have to give Stewart an answer before you leave. You at least owe him a phone call."

"I'll call him. I just don't know what to tell him right now."

Seeing the anguish in his face, Wendy moved toward him, wrapped her arms around his body and gazed up into his eyes. "Honey, just tell him the truth. He'll respect that. And you know I'll support you regardless of the decision you make. I love you so much, honey." Wendy rested her head against his chest. "I'm really sorry I lost it yesterday, Troy. But I miss you so darn much when you're not here."

Troy gently cupped her face in his hands, and kissed her tenderly on the lips. "I know, darling. I love you so very much, too."

Troy's mind raced in frustration. He couldn't tell Wendy what was going on, even though she deserved to know. Yet at this point he really didn't know much more than what he'd already told her. In a way, he was thankful that Colonel Sparks hadn't given the crews any more information. All he knew for sure was that they were going to Eglin to fly B-47s.

He sighed. *I'll just have to take each day one at a time; that's all I can do right now,* he thought. His main concern was for Wendy and her pregnancy.

The five days at home went by too swiftly. SAC had arranged for a KC-135 to transport them to Eglin. Wendy, Gail and Beth came to base-ops to see them off. Colonel Blauw also stopped by to wish them well.

Chapter XII

As TROY AND HIS crew climbed down from the tanker at Eglin AFB, heavy, humid air and the pungent smell of Gulf seawater immediately filled their nostrils. Tiny, biting flies encircled their bodies and seemed determined to move in unison with them. It was a stark change from the pleasant Southern California atmosphere they had just left.

While checking into the BOQ, Troy picked up a brochure relating the history of the base. He learned that Eglin AFB opened in the mid-1930s as a bombing and gunnery range for the newly formed Army Air Corps. With ten active airfields at the northwest Florida base, Eglin encompassed more acreage than any other facility in the Air Force. During World War II, the base served as a test range for aircraft tactics and new equipment and was the primary training site for Doolittle's B-25 Tokyo Raiders.

Troy and his crew spent the first training day getting to know their instructors and participating in flight planning for the pilots' local orientation flight. Troy's first impression of his instructor, a civilian pilot named Charles Enloe, was that he was a pleasant and very quiet fellow. With more than two thousand hours in the B-47, Enloe seemed well qualified for this high-performance training.

Enloe was in his late thirties, stood at five feet six, with sculpted facial features, and graying, close-cropped hair. He had been in the B-47 program from its infancy and was one of SAC's first professional instructor pilots. When Boeing needed qualified B-47 pilots for its government contracts, the company offered Enloe enough money to lure him away from the Air Force.

With Troy in front and Enloe behind him in the copilot's seat, the two of them taxied onto the runway for Troy's orientation flight.

"Okay, Bench," Enloe's voice rasped over the interphone, "let's see how fast you can pull this thing off the runway. We're light, with only thirty-five thousand pounds of gas, so show me how you Academy boys can fly."

Troy was surprised by the inappropriate tone of the comment, especially with six jet engines turning at 100 percent and the plane within seconds of thundering down the runway. Was Enloe intentionally trying to harass him and make him nervous, or did he just dislike Academy grads? Troy didn't have time to deal with the commentary, so he let it pass. "Sir, I'll lift it off as the computed takeoff data calls for," he said in a calm but authoritative voice.

After lifting off and retracting the gear and flaps, Troy set climb power at 310 knots. At twenty thousand feet heading south over the Gulf of Mexico, Enloe barked his first airborne command. "Okay, flyboy, give me a sixty-degree bank to the right, and then one to the left." SAC regulations specifically restricted the B-47 to a max forty-five-degree bank, partly because of the angle of its swept wings. Troy sensed the hostility and angst in Enloe's voice, but he couldn't think of anything he had said or done that may have brought it on. Enloe had been such a pleasant person during flight planning the previous day. Why had he now turned into this verbal antagonist?

For a moment, Troy hesitated to follow Enloe's instructions.

"All right, goddammit! Let go of the airplane!" Enloe barked gruffly. "Let me show you how to fly this thing. Now watch closely and follow through with me."

Troy observed how precisely Enloe executed the sixty-degree banking turns while providing continuous verbal instruction throughout. The altimeter never varied more than eighty feet, nor did the airspeed move more than a few knots. Troy was impressed; he had to admit the guy was damned good.

"Okay, you think you can do that? You got the airplane, Bench. Give me two 360s with a sixty-degree bank."

Troy muscled the bomber into a steep bank while keeping the airspeed within 15 knots and not letting the altitude vary more than a couple hundred feet.

"Okay, Bench, that's not bad," Enloe said calmly, but Troy could sense the contempt in his voice.

For the next two hours, Enloe put Troy through a series of maneuvers that pushed the airplane's performance to the razor's edge: diving the big bomber from twenty-five thousand feet at 425 knots, leveling off at two hundred to three hundred feet above the water, then hauling back on the yoke while pulling positive Gs all the way up to altitude, and culminating the series at the top with an Immelman-type maneuver.

The exercises gave Troy the aerial workout of his life. He would have bet that only a handful of B-47 pilots had ever thought of, much less performed, the outer-limit maneuvers. Given the circumstances, Troy felt he'd done well. Toward the end of the flight Enloe's demeanor seemed less abrasive, but he continued to refer to him as "Academy Boy." If he was trying to antagonize him, it hadn't worked. Troy was proud of having been in the first class to graduate from the Air

Force Academy. He didn't like Enloe's attitude, but he wasn't going to let it get to him. Besides, he had to admit he'd learned a lot from the little bastard.

Later, during ground debriefing, Enloe's personality did an about-face. He returned to being the courteous, pleasant person Troy had met the previous day and referred to him throughout the debriefing as Captain Bench.

That evening at the club over a beer with Mangino and Candee, Troy described the flight and the verbal harassment Enloe have given him. "Shit, let me at that little son of a bitch," Bill Candee said. "I'll straighten his ass out real quick. Just give me the word, Troy."

"I can handle it," Troy assured his crew. "He's the one with the problem, not me. I'll figure him out in due time."

Candee and Mangino joined Troy on the next couple of training flights, which concentrated on low-level, overwater navigation; ELINT (electronic intelligence); and ECM (electronic countermeasures). Ultra top-secret ECM and ELINT black boxes as well as larger chaff dispensers, used to thwart enemy radars, had been installed on the Eglin airplanes. On the second flight, an instructor navigator gave Mangino a workout utilizing a newly installed radar altimeter that had an auxiliary scope at the aircraft commander position. A forward-looking radar antenna had been integrated into the MA-7 radar system to enhance the bomb-nav's view of landmasses at a greater distance while at low altitude.

An EWO (electronic warfare officer) instructor flew with the crew on the third mission, evaluating the bomb-nav's and copilot's use of the newly installed EW equipment. Candee and Mangino successfully deciphered and separated the cryptic signals of the various Soviet-style ground-based and airborne radars that were aimed at them from the Eglin test range. It was crucial that the crew be able to instantly detect the type of radars painting them, so that they could quickly choose which electronic countermeasures to activate and which evasive action to take. An error in judgment or even a few seconds' delay in activating countermeasures could cost them their lives.

On the fourth and fifth training flights, Enloe instructed the full crew. It was the first time Mangino and Candee had been on a flight with him. With Candee in the copilot seat, Enloe in the aircraft commander position, Troy in the fourth-man seat, and Mangino in the nose, they leveled off at twenty-six thousand feet.

"Okay, Candee, follow me through on a sixty-degree banking turn," Enloe ordered.

Candee was obviously impressed with Enloe's flying skills. "Damn, man! You fly a pretty shit-hot airplane," Candee blurted out over the interphone.

"All right, let's see what you've learned. Give me a 360 with a 60-degree bank," Enloe commanded.

Candee stalled and fell out of the turn before reaching 45 degrees of bank. Enloe grabbed the airplane and recovered. "Now, goddammit, instead of running your mouth, follow through with me and listen this time."

Candee, visibly shaken and angered by his inability to perform the maneuver, was determined to make it work. He rolled the airplane into a 60-degree bank and held it throughout 720 degrees of turn. The altitude varied only a few hundred feet and the airspeed by maybe thirty knots.

"That's better," Enloe barked. "It's important you be able to help your aircraft commander in these maneuvers if he gets into trouble or has his hands full with something else. You understand me?"

"Yes, sir, I do." Candee's meek response was completely out of character.

After a series of high-speed dives from altitude to low-level with max-performance pull-ups, Candee's performance improved. When Candee glanced down at Troy in the fourth-man position, Troy flashed him a smile that said, "*Now* you understand what I've been going through!"

"All right, Candee," Enloe said over the interphone. "Let's see how you can operate those twenty-millimeter cannons in the tail."

Candee swiveled his seat 180 degrees and performed a series of firing exercises using the A-5 radar fire control system. The gun-laying system in the B-47 was unreliable; most of the time it didn't work, and when it did, it wasn't very accurate. However, the Soviets didn't know that. The mere thought of guns in the tail of the bomber tended to discourage Soviet fighters from making a tail-on pass, which was their most desirable tactic for a kill.

Later, during Enloe's ground debriefing, Candee was silent until the end. Stepping closer to Enloe so that their faces were just a few inches apart, Candee spoke in his best West Texas twang. "I gotta tell ya, man, you are one shit-hot pilot."

Enloe merely gave a slight nod of his head. "I'll see you all tomorrow," he said and walked away.

After he departed, Candee whispered, "There goes one arrogant son of a bitch."

As SAC project officer for Shark Bite operations, Colonel Sparks had come down from Omaha to fly with each of the eight crews. Troy was first. With Sparks in the backseat, they were taxiing out on mission number six when he asked Troy if he could make the takeoff to maintain his B-47 proficiency. Troy was impressed with Sparks's pilot skills throughout the flight, especially considering that flying wasn't a primary duty for a headquarters guy. During the debriefing Sparks asked if anyone had any questions.

"Yes, sir. Can you tell us any more about our follow-on assignment, and more specifically, what we're going to be doing?" Troy asked.

"A briefer from SAC will be here at the end of the week. He'll answer most of your questions. Is there anything else you'd like to discuss with me while you've got me cornered?"

"No, sir, and I want to thank you for flying with us," Troy responded. "I learned a lot. You fly a nice airplane."

"Sir, if you don't mind," Candee interrupted, "I have a question. Let's see if I can put this tactfully … Oh, hell, I'll just say it my way. You mentioned you'd known Enloe for a long time. Has he always been such an asshole?"

"Lieutenant, you're darn lucky to have had Charlie Enloe as your IP. He's one of the finest pilots ever to touch the yoke of a B-47. He can do things with this airplane most B-47 pilots only dream about. Yes, he may be a bit gruff—that's his nature—but he grows on you. Anything else, gentlemen?"

"No, sir, and thank you again. It's been a pleasure flying with you, Colonel."

"It's mutual. You've got a fine crew, Bench."

Several days later, during debriefing of their final training flight, Enloe surprised Troy and his crew by inviting them to his home in Fort Walton Beach for dinner. Troy borrowed a car from one of the other crews and drove them to where Enloe and his wife, Isabelle, lived a block from the beach. On the way, Troy cautioned Candee to be on his best behavior. "Remember, we're guests."

"I'll try my best, Troy," Candee promised.

Isabelle Enloe answered the door, introducing herself and inviting them inside. "Let me guess. You're Troy," she said, flawless white teeth accentuating her gracious smile. Isabelle was a stunning woman, about five feet four, with dark hair, smooth Florida-bronzed skin, and a trim body. Troy was surprised that this outgoing woman was married to the introverted Enloe.

"Yes, ma'am," Troy said, reaching out to shake her hand. "I'm pleased to meet you."

Isabelle then pointed toward Joe. "And you're Joe Mangino."

"You're very good, ma'am." Mangino reached for her hand.

"And this one's easy," she said when she came to Candee. "You're Bill Candee, the handsome Texan."

"Well, thank you, ma'am," Candee said. "I see my reputation precedes me."

Wearing a bright yellow Hawaiian shirt and cream-colored slacks, Charlie Enloe entered the room. With a broad, hospitable smile that none of the crew members had ever seen before, Enloe shook everyone's hands and welcomed them to his home.

After an exchange of pleasantries, Isabelle suggested that Charlie show the crew his patio arboretum while she finished preparing the meal.

As they walked through the house and back outside, Troy found himself in an explosion of color. Hundreds of rare and exotic tropical plants thrived in every corner of the high, walled-in backyard. Enloe beamed with pride as he walked his guests through the area, describing each of the South and Central American plants and expounding on their origins and Latin and generic names. His botanical accomplishments revealed a soft, introspective side of Charlie Enloe that Troy had never seen before.

After Enloe finished with his tour, he passed out cans of beer from a cooler and the men shared flying stories. Troy excused himself to go inside and use the bathroom. Passing through the kitchen on his way back out, he asked Isabelle if there was anything he could do to help.

"I'm almost finished with the salad and the corn on the cob, but I wouldn't mind a little company. Why don't you sit down and visit?" Isabelle said with a smile. "You know, I probably shouldn't tell you this, Troy, but I will anyway. Charlie's a little gruff at times—I'm sure you know that by now—but the man has a heart of gold. And he thinks the world of you and your crew."

Troy tried to keep his surprise from showing as

Isabelle stacked plates and silverware on the counter. "He's taken a special interest in you that I've never seen before," she continued. "Says he doesn't know where you're headed, but he has a pretty good idea of what you're going to be doing. He told me he could never forgive himself if anything happened and it was due to something he had missed in his flight instruction."

"Thank you for sharing that, ma'am. Because of your husband, I've learned how to fly this airplane to its limits."

"By the way, you're an Academy grad, aren't you, Troy?"

"Yes, ma'am, I am."

"Our son, Mark, started at the Academy about the same year you graduated, but he dropped out after a year. Decided military life wasn't for him. About broke his father's heart. Charlie blamed both the Academy and Mark. He felt the Academy should have done more to retain him." Isabelle paused, a frown darkening her features. "Next year our son graduates from Purdue in engineering. But the relationship between Mark and his dad still remains strained because of that experience."

"I'm sorry I didn't know him, ma'am. He sounds like a fine young man."

The evening was delightful. It was interspersed

with stories of Enloe's Air Force career and, of course, many flying stories.

As Troy and his crew prepared to leave later in the evening, they shared warm handshakes and hugs all around. Troy thought he saw Enloe's eyes grow damp as he wished each crew member the best of luck and Godspeed. Troy couldn't help but wonder whether Charles Malos Enloe still wished he had a pilot son. Could it be? He was thankful that Isabelle had related the story about their son. It cleared up a huge mystery for the "Academy Boy."

....

All eight crews came to attention as Major General Marvin Miller strode to the podium at a hastily called briefing at Eglin. As deputy director for plans and programs at SAC headquarters, Miller was Colonel Sparks's boss.

"Gentlemen, I personally wanted to come down here and congratulate all of you on completing one of the toughest flight training programs any bomber crew has ever undergone. I'm sure you'll agree with me on that." Miller paused to meet the smiles of acknowledgment from the crew members. "I also wanted to thank you for your patience during the past month. I realize that not knowing what you were going to be doing and where you were going to be doing it has been trying for both you and your families. Well, that's over now. Let me introduce Brigadier

General Gordon Spaulding, deputy director for intelligence at SAC."

"Good morning, gentlemen. I want to add my congratulations to those of General Miller on completion of a difficult flight training program. You've learned to do things with the B-47 that most people would quake in their boots even thinking about. You've also proved that young, low-flying-time crews *can* operate this aircraft at its outer limits. You can be proud of yourselves. Gentlemen, you're an extremely valuable SAC asset right now."

The congratulatory mood took a serious turn as the general leaned in and looked intently at the crew members. "What I'm about to tell you is highly classified and is to be treated as such. As some of you may know, we've been penetrating Soviet airspace for several years. We've occasionally lost airplanes and crews on these missions. Most of the overflights were conducted by the Air Force, a few by the Navy. SAC's RB-47 reconnaissance crews from Forbes and Lockbourne Air Force Bases have performed the bulk of this dangerous work.

"However, the Soviets have recently wised up to our tactics. They've moved their advanced MiG-17 fighters around their border perimeters, which has made it difficult to obtain valuable electronic intelligence. As bomber crews, you know how important it is to have the latest intelligence on your assigned wartime targets. We *must* have continuous electronic intelligence updates to keep our war plans current. The Soviets know we're after that electronic data. So they've stopped turning on their SAMs—their surface-to-air missiles—and gun-laying, antiaircraft radars when we perform our overflights with reconnaissance aircraft.

"Gentlemen, we think that by using bombers to penetrate their coastlines—rather than reconnaissance aircraft—we'll create sufficient threat uncertainty in the Soviets' minds. This will provoke them into turning on their defensive electronic equipment. Our ELINT aircraft orbiting at a safe distance farther out to sea will be standing by to acquire this valuable signal intelligence.

"With this information, we can then develop countermeasures that will be integrated into our war plans."

Candee leaned toward Troy. "Holy crap!" he whispered. "What the hell are we in for, boss? This is going to be exciting, all right."

"Gentlemen, you will be provided with more detailed information upon arrival at your OL."

The general then flashed a slide listing assignments onto a screen behind him. Troy saw his name at the top of the slide: "BENCH—Operating Location, Eielson AFB, Fairbanks, Alaska."

Four crews were assigned to Eielson, the other four to Royal Air Force Base, Brize Norton, England.

"Gentlemen, what you've heard here today is classified as top secret, need-to-know. The key is 'need to know.' Few people are cleared for this information—only a handful even at SAC headquarters. Your wives, girlfriends, and even your commanders are not cleared. That's why you've been provided with a cover story and the unclassified code name, Shark Bite. Your cover story is that you will be conducting overwater, low-level testing for B-47s. I must advise you that anyone violating any part of this *trusted* information will be prosecuted to the limit of the law. Is that clearly understood?"

The crew members nodded in silence. There were no questions.

"I know you've been away from your families for almost a month. And I know you'd like to get home for some R&R. However, because of SAC's urgent need for this information, you've been authorized only three days at your home base. You'll then return to Eglin and fly your aircraft to your designated OL. I suggest you use this time to get your personal affairs in order before reporting back to Eglin.

"As Colonel Sparks advised you weeks ago, the missions you are about to undertake are not going to be easy—they could be dangerous. Be assured, you've been provided with the best training possible. And we think you're ready.

"Gentlemen, we're going to be watching your daily operations very closely at SAC headquarters. We're depending on you. So, good luck, good flying, and Godspeed."

Chapter XIII

TROY HAD BEEN DESIGNATED force commander, with the responsibility of leading the formation of four Shark B-47s from Eglin to Eielson AFB, Alaska, a distance of more than thirty-five hundred miles. Because of predicted strong jet-stream headwinds slowing their progress, North Dakota Air Guard tankers refueled the aircraft as they crossed the border into Canada. Flying at thirty-eight thousand feet in one-mile trail formation with altitude separation of five hundred feet, the formation tracked across the snow-covered frozen tundra of the Alberta and Yukon Territories. Entering Alaska near the mouth of the Tanana River, made famous during Alaskan gold-rush days, Troy ordered Sharks 02, 03, and 04 to establish a five-mile separation for approach and landing at Eielson AFB.

Eielson Approach Control advised Troy of moderate to severe turbulence below twenty thousand feet, shifting westerly winds with gusts up to thirty knots, blowing snow, moderate runway icing conditions, and a ground temperature of -38 degrees. Candee transmitted the landing information to all Shark aircraft with the comment, "Welcome to our new winter vacation land."

Landing on runway thirty-one, Troy slammed the aircraft hard on the icy surface as an Arctic gust jerked the left outrigger off the ground. Cranking in full left aileron, he forced the outrigger back onto the runway. Candee immediately deployed the brake chute, which slowed the bomber and stopped it from sliding toward the right side of the slippery runway. The antiskid brakes further slowed the aircraft, and Troy was able to turn off at the last exit.

With his oxygen mask unhooked and dangling across his face, Troy peered into the inky darkness. "Are we on the right taxiway, Bill?"

"Off to your right, boss. You see the FOLLOW-ME truck?"

"Yeah, got him now. Thanks."

"That was one hell of a landing," Candee said. "Good job."

Troy pressed his mike button. "Eielson Tower, this is Shark Zero-one. You need to advise follow-on Shark aircraft to be alert for turbulent winds with strong gusts and an icy runway."

"Roger, Zero-one, I'll advise them immediately."

The other three crews soon landed safely in spite

of the challenging conditions. At debriefing, they were informed of an eight o'clock meeting the following morning with Colonel Sparks. SAC had designated Sparks as the OL commander, responsible for Pacific Shark Bite operations.

....

Four B-47 crews took their seats in the briefing room of a windowless, single-floor, concrete structure known as the Blockhouse. The building served as the north Pacific's nerve center for reconnaissance and intelligence activities.

"Gentlemen, welcome to Eielson Air Force Base," Colonel Sparks said as he welcomed the Shark Bite crews. "I hope your quarters are comfortable and that you had a good night's sleep. Before I get started on the mission briefing this morning, I want to give you a little background info on Eielson and the surrounding area.

"As you probably know, we bought Alaska from the Russians in the mid-nineteenth century. But it wasn't until 1959 that it became our forty-ninth state. In the early twentieth century, the discovery of gold and other minerals made Alaska attractive to settlers, and the village of Fairbanks was established in the Tanana River Valley, where we are now. Eielson was activated toward the end of World War II as a refueling and staging facility for lend-lease aircraft we were flying into Russia to help them in their fight against the Nazis."

Troy's mind darted to the irony of the situation. *Now here we are, planning to carry out reconnaissance missions against a former ally.*

Sparks continued. "Eielson is home to a squadron of fighter interceptors, KC-135 tankers, and a half dozen B-47s on reflex alert. While you're here, the Blockhouse will be command central for your flight operations.

"Tomorrow, gentlemen, you'll fly a five-hour orientation mission toward the Bering Sea, terminating with a simulated low-level attack on Kodiak Island. We've scheduled your takeoff for 11:00 AM to take advantage of the few hours of daylight we have at this time of year. You'll be happy to hear that the temperature is supposed to reach 6 degrees tomorrow—a real heat wave.

"I want you to keep in mind as you fly these missions that the Soviet's long-range EW radars will monitor your every airborne move. Tomorrow we'll start establishing a pattern for them to track. We want to keep them on their toes. With each mission we'll work our way farther west.

"Now for the good news. A bus will pick you up in front of your quarters at noon today and take you into Fairbanks. You can explore the town until four o'clock, then head for the Klondike Saloon; we've reserved tables there. This establishment has the finest steaks west of Kansas City. It's a rowdy place, so watch yourselves. Enjoy the day, gentlemen. You've got some hard flying ahead of you."

Colonel Sparks had arranged for a small room in the crew's quarters with a desk, a comfortable chair, and a telephone with a landline to the States. Crews were authorized to use it at any time to call their families. It proved to be an essential morale booster.

Troy finally got through to Wendy after several failed attempts. "Hi, honey. How are ya doing?"

"Oh, Troy, I'm so glad to hear your voice. I'm just fine, hon. How was your flight?"

"Had a rough landing, but otherwise it was uneventful."

"Troy, I had an appointment with my doctor yesterday. He said the baby's coming along just fine, and my weight is perfect. I also think I'm about over my morning sickness." Troy was glad to hear the good news. "Mom came to the doctor with me, and then we went shopping for baby stuff. It was late when we got home, so she stayed over. We talked until almost midnight. It was really great!" Troy was pleased that Wendy's mom lived nearby.

"That's good news about the baby. Bet your mom's really happy to be close enough to drive over. And it makes me feel a lot better to know your parents are close by."

"Troy, before I forget, I need to tell you something. There's a rumor going around March that you guys are doing more than just testing B-47s up there—that you're involved in some kind of secret project. I called Mark yesterday, and he told me to ignore the rumors. Said some folks with too much time on their hands were spreading gossip. But I don't know how to react if someone approaches me about it. What should I say, Troy?"

Troy froze, not knowing exactly how to answer. He couldn't lie to Wendy, but he couldn't tell her the truth either. "Honey, Mark was right," he said after a few seconds of silence. "Don't listen to the rumors. We're doing the job we were sent here to do."

"Okay, that's what I'll say if anyone asks. I just thought you ought to know."

"I'm glad you told me," Troy said and glanced down at his watch. "Honey, I've got to run. A bus is taking us into Fairbanks for an evening on the town. We're having dinner at the Klondike Saloon." Troy paused, reluctant to end the call. "Sweetie, I love you so much, and I miss you. I'll talk with you tomorrow."

"I miss you, too, Troy. Have a great evening in Fairbanks. I love you, darling."

....

The Klondike Saloon lived up to its reputation. Troy found a unique charm in the rusticity of its shadowy décor, the stench of stale beer, the aging wooden walls bearing more than seventy-five years of hand-carved girls' phone numbers, and the pine floors covered in peanut shells, sawdust, and dirt. The steaks also lived up to their advance billing.

The evening provided an atmosphere for a closer bonding of the group. Between swills of dark beer and the comforting rumble of other diners, Troy found himself enjoying his discussions with the other crew members taking part in these unique and dangerous missions.

The arduous training they had endured, and the uncertainty of what lay ahead, established an *esprit* and a strong camaraderie among the fliers. They were eager to get on with their missions, to complete the job SAC had sent them to do, and to return home to their families.

The following day a two-ship formation, with Troy in the lead and Tom Reed's crew as number two, flew the first leg of their mission to Nome, only 150 miles from the Soviet coastline. They tweaked the Soviet EW radars, and then cut sharply south to Cold Bay on the Aleutian chain. They then turned northeast and descended to low-level, executing a pop-up simulated bomb run on Kodiak Airfield.

On the leg back to Eielson, Mangino pressed his mike button. "God, what a gorgeous day and what a beautiful state Alaska is! I gotta tell ya, though, I'd hate to punch out over this frozen landmass and even less into that choppy ocean below us. I can see chunks of ice floating around down there. Bet you'd last only a few minutes in that stuff."

Troy and Candee echoed Mangino's thoughts.

....

The crews soon settled into a routine of flight planning one day and flying the next. In the middle of flight planning for mission two, Colonel Sparks called the crews into the briefing room for an intelligence update.

"Gentlemen, you remember Lieutenant Colonel Stan Zuko from the Directorate of Intelligence at SAC. Colonel Zuko has an update on the activities of our sister Shark Bite crews at RAF Brize Norton."

Colonel Zuko, a soft-spoken career intelligence officer, had spent the last eighteen years of his Air Force career studying Soviet electronic intelligence activities as well as E&E, or escape-and-evasion, techniques for SAC crew members.

"Good morning, gentlemen. I'm sure you've been wondering how your friends in the other half of the Shark Bite operation are doing. Since they started flying a day earlier, they're one mission ahead of us. Yesterday, they embarked on their second mission with Captain Markey in the lead and Captain Tacke as number two. The crews flew to within twenty-five miles of the heavily defended target city of Murmansk on the Barents Sea. At that point they were jumped by what they believed were four MiG-21s. According to prearranged tactics and rules of engagement, the formation split with Markey taking a northerly heading out over the Barents Sea and Tacke a more westerly track across the northern tip of Finland." Zuko paused momentarily to check the reaction of the crew members, but there were no questions.

Continuing, "The MiGs did not pursue either B-47 and, to the best of the crews' knowledge, no shots were fired. It may have been that the MiGs weren't armed, they could have been low on fuel, or it's possible their commanders may have been too surprised and confused to issue orders to engage. Whatever the case, we can't count on being that lucky again. Both airplanes landed safely at Brize.

"The crews estimated that the MiGs approached to within three miles. They positioned themselves on either side of the formation rather than closing from the rear. Our best guess is that the MiG pilots were aware of the cannons in the tail of the B-47s and cautiously avoided that potential cone of danger.

"The mission was an intelligence success in that our standoff ELINT aircraft picked up some new and valuable surface-to-air missile and fire-control radar signals. Gentlemen, that's all the info I have at the present time. Are there any questions?"

Mangino raised his hand. "Sir, were the Shark aircraft at low altitude or high?"

"They were high, at thirty-nine thousand feet. Any

more questions?" Observing the silence, the colonel switched gears. "If not, then I want to talk to you about another subject. You've all been through the rugged two-week Air Force Survival School near Spokane. While there, you learned E&E tactics and were taught the nuts and bolts of the code of conduct and actions expected of you as a POW. For most of you, this training took place a couple of years ago. So, I've scheduled a refresher session this evening on E&E procedures and the code. I'll see you all back here at five o'clock."

Taking off at 10:00 AM the following day, Troy and his crew flew mission two over Kodiak Island and headed westward along the fog-shrouded Aleutian chain toward Attu.

Candee broke the familiar silence with a hesitant question. "Boss, what do you think it'd be like to have MiGs sitting off our wing?"

"I'm not sure, but we may soon find out," Troy answered grimly.

"Bill, that reminds me, I want you to start practicing how quickly you can swivel that seat of yours 180 degrees and change from copilot to tail gunner. If we come across any MiGs, our survival may depend on how fast you can get those radar-controlled cannons working. A couple of blasts from our twenty-millimeters could keep them at bay and discourage 'em from lining up on our tail. Another thing, I want you to put the guns in standby when we get within two hundred miles of the Soviet mainland. Got it?"

"Count on it, boss," said Candee.

Mangino mashed his floor interphone switch. "Hey guys, if you look off to your right you can see the tiny island of Shemya. That and Misawa in northern Japan are our only authorized emergency landing fields. Get a good look. It's unusual for Shemya to be clear this time of year." Troy hoped he'd never have to use that postage stamp of a runway in an emergency. "I pity the poor bastards down there who have to maintain and operate that early-warning equipment. They've got forty-mile-per-hour freezing winds howling at them every day. You've got to have screwed up big-time to land a one-year assignment on that rock.

"Troy, you can start a right turn now to heading 060—that'll take us home. By the way, if you look down during the turn you'll see the thirty-five-mile-long island of Attu of World War II fame. Some of the bloodiest fighting of the war, second only to Iwo Jima, took place on that island."

"Thanks for the history lesson, Joe," Candee said. "Sure looks like a godforsaken rock to me. It must have had some strategic value back then."

Candee paused and then shared another thought. "I wonder how we'd feel if Soviet bombers were trolling our coastlines like we're doing theirs."

"In the first place," Troy answered, "how do you

know they're not? And second, they don't *need* to ferret out our electronic data. With our open society, they can get all the intel they need from *Aviation Week* or through their spy network."

"Hey, gang. We just crossed the international date line," Mangino announced. "We've gone from today into tomorrow, and now we're back to today again."

"That's too complicated for an old Texas boy," Candee said. "Glad the date line doesn't run through Lubbock. My ranch hands would go nuts trying to figure out that stuff."

"I just tucked us into a 170-mile-per-hour jet stream," Mangino said. "The tailwind's giving us a ground speed of almost seven hundred miles per hour. That'll get us home a half hour early."

"Good, I need to call Wendy before it gets too late," Troy said.

....

"Hi, Wendy. How are you and the baby doing?"

"Oh, hi Troy. I'm doing fine. The baby's kicking a lot now. How was the flight?"

"Piece of cake. Did your mom come by today?"

"Yeah, we went to a movie. We just finished dinner. Think she's going to spend the night."

"What was the name of it—the movie, I mean?"

"I don't remember, Troy. I was thinking about you the whole time. Are you doing okay?"

"Honey, I'm doing just fine. Stop worrying. We're

having a wonderful time—playing handball, reading—everything's great. But I hate being away from you." Troy shifted the phone to his other ear. "By the way, I think Joe may have a bug or something. He was feeling a bit under the weather after we landed today. I told him to go see the flight surgeon in the morning."

"That's too bad. Will they give you another bomb-nav?"

"Yeah, probably. I'll have to wait and see if he's grounded. Don't say anything to Gail, though. Let him tell her. Honey, I'd better get to bed and let you go to bed, too. I've got a big one to fly tomorrow. I love you so much and I miss you terribly."

"Oh, Troy, I miss you too. I just wish you were here so you could hold me. Honey, please be careful and hurry home. I love you, my darling. Good night."

After replacing the receiver in its cradle, Wendy sat down in the kitchen chair, her stomach churning nervously. Her fear must have been visible on her face because her mother rushed to her in concern.

"What is it, honey? What's wrong?" her mother asked.

"I don't know, but I'm afraid." Wendy paused and looked up at her mother. "Something's going on that Troy's not telling me. Mom, I'm scared."

Chapter XIV

GENERAL STRONG, SAC'S COMMANDER in chief, had received daily intelligence updates and progress reports from the Shark Bite operations at Eielson and Brize Norton. He was pleased with the intel data that had been acquired so far, but a briefing on the MiG incident left him concerned for the safety of his crews.

SAC headquarters transmitted new, top-secret guidance on rules of engagement to all Shark Bite crews. "If approached by MiGs, do not provoke them. Turn away and exit the area immediately. You are authorized to return fire if fired upon and to take evasive action as deemed necessary and prudent for safety of your crew and aircraft."

....

At breakfast, Mangino still had a hacking cough, bloodshot eyes, and a sore throat. "I'll be just fine,

Troy," he insisted. "I promise I'll check in with the flight surgeon after we land tomorrow."

Troy's response was swift and firm. "Joe, I appreciate your dedication, but I can't jeopardize the mission, nor will I put your health in danger. I want you to go see the flight surgeon. If he says you're okay, then you can fly. Otherwise, you can join us on the next mission."

Later that morning, Troy and Candee walked the short distance to the Blockhouse through a blizzard of swirling ice crystals that stung their faces. Colonel Sparks met them at the entrance. "Just got a call from the flight surgeon—Mangino's grounded. It's nothing serious, but the doc wants to keep him in the hospital overnight for observation. Since Tom Reed's crew won't be flying for the next couple of days, I'm assigning his bomb-nav to you for this mission. Lieutenant Carl Olson is on his way over."

A tight end on the Air Force Academy football team, Carl had been a classmate of Troy's. He was well over six feet tall, with a wiry muscular build and thinning blond hair. A bright individual, Carl graduated twenty-second in his class of 207. For the last three years, he had been the bomb-nav on Tom Reed's B-47 crew at Dyess AFB, Texas.

"Hey, Troy, looks like we're flying together," Carl said, easing his lanky frame into a gray metal flight-planning chair.

"Looks that way, Carl; Joe went sick on us. Welcome aboard. You know Bill Candee?"

Candee reached across the table and shook Carl's hand. "We've met. Welcome to the crew, Carl. This is really a red-letter day for me. Here I am, an old Texas Tech Red Raider flying with a couple of sophisticated Air Force Academy grads. Wowee! I'll try to boost my Texas intellect a couple of notches so as not to embarrass you guys."

Troy and Carl laughed. "That's okay, Bill," Troy said good-naturedly. "We acknowledge your handicap, but we're willing to work with you."

Troy and Carl reminisced about some of their Academy classmates. Then, Troy leaned forward with an inquisitive grin. "Carl, there's something I gotta ask you. Been thinking about this since we were at Eglin. At the Academy, you dated one of the cutest girls in all of Colorado—a blonde, great body, and smart, too. If I remember, her name was Linda, and I believe she was going to Denver University. Do ya know what ever happened to her?"

Carl laughed with obvious pleasure. "That pretty blonde's my wife, Troy, and I think it was you who introduced us! We were married right after graduation. We have two of the most beautiful little girls you ever saw—Megan and Sara. They look just like Linda."

"That's great, Carl. Doubt if Linda would remember me, but pass on my regards, anyway."

"Oh, she'll remember you. While we were dating, I can't tell you how many times she asked me, 'Who's that cute Troy going with now?' Think she had a bit of a crush on you."

"Well, I'm flattered. And congratulations on those beautiful girls."

....

Lieutenant Colonel Zuko and his intel people had designed mission three to skirt the Soviet's Kamchatka Peninsula. Geographically, the Kamchatka landmass began about five hundred miles south of the Arctic Circle and extended roughly seven hundred miles farther south, with its eastern shoreline facing the Bering Sea. Because of its strategic location, Kamchatka held great military significance for the Soviets, and thus tremendous interest for the intel folks at SAC headquarters.

The peninsula was loaded with airfields and brimming with long-range bombers and MiG-17, 19, and 21 fighter/intercept aircraft. The landmass also contained intercontinental ballistic missile sites that were programmed for launch toward the United States. Additionally, it was headquarters for the Soviet's massive Pacific submarine fleet. Kamchatka was so highly classified by the Soviets that foreigners and even most Russians were banned from visiting the area.

Colonel Zuko handed out prepared maps for mission number three, annotated with headings, distances, and times, to Troy and his crew. He explained that the mission would be a single-ship, solo flight so as not to excessively antagonize the Soviets. SAC wanted to needle them just enough to obtain the required intelligence.

Takeoff was scheduled for 9:30 AM to take advantage of the minimal daylight conditions over the target areas. Radio silence would be maintained throughout the flight except for an emergency Mayday-type situation.

Troy, Carl, and Candee reviewed every detail of the route and discussed contingencies they might encounter along the way. Troy knew this might be one of the most exacting missions he would fly, and he stressed this upon his crew. From Eielson, they would proceed on a westerly heading toward Norton Sound on Alaska's west coast. There, an Alaskan National Guard tanker would top them off with twenty thousand pounds of fuel. They would then fly to the south tip of Saint Lawrence Island, turn on a track of 250 degrees, and skirt the Soviet coastline to the Olyutorskiy Peninsula. If they hadn't aroused Soviet defenses by then, they would proceed on a more southerly heading to Kamchatskiy Point, midway down the peninsula, and then turn eastward toward Attu and back to Eielson.

The route would place them directly over Soviet

territory for no more than five to eight minutes. But for almost two hours they would be within ten to fifty miles of the Soviet coastline. Intel hoped that the close proximity of the bomber for that period of time would trigger the Soviets into turning on their search, height-finder, and fire-control radars for their highly sophisticated surface-to-air missile and intercept air defense systems. Prepositioned ELINT aircraft would be standing by some fifty to seventy miles out, listening to record every frequency and sound of the Soviet electronic systems.

Zuko emphasized that at any point along the route, were Troy and his crew threatened by SAMs or MiGs, they should immediately turn on an easterly, nonthreatening track and head for home, as per the new rules of engagement.

Zuko updated the crew on the Brize Norton Shark mission three. "The flights took place over the Kara Sea area some seventy miles northeast of Murmansk. No MiGs or SAMs were encountered, and only minimal Soviet defensive radars had been energized."

Troy asked about the significance of the Soviet inaction.

"They may have guessed what we're trying to do and decided not to buy into it, but we really don't know," Zuko explained.

On the way back to their quarters, Troy and Candee stopped off at the small base hospital to check on Mangino. He seemed to be in fine shape, with several civilian nurses' aides fussing over him and trying to get him to eat. When Mangino saw Troy and Candee in the doorway, he shooed the nurses out with a couple of mild expletives.

"Well, I see you've ingratiated your charming self to the staff," Candee said dryly. "You better be nice to those folks. You may need 'em in the middle of the night."

"Oh hell, I'm just fine. They're driving me nuts," Mangino grumbled. "How'd the flight planning go? And who's replacing me?"

After Troy brought him up to date, Mangino nodded in approval. "Carl's a good guy—he'll get you there and back safely. I'm glad he's flying with you. I'm just mad as hell that I got this damn flu bug. By the way, guys, you probably ought to get out of here before you get it, too."

As Troy and Candee said their good-byes and moved to leave, Mangino stopped them. "Hey, promise you'll give me a call when you land. I want to know how things went, okay?"

"We'll do it," Troy assured him.

Chapter XV

A HIGH LAYER OF cirrocumulus clouds was Troy's only reminder of yesterday's ice storm. Shark Zero-one departed from runway three-one at Eielson and headed for a silent airborne rendezvous and refueling with an Alaskan Air Guard tanker.

Carl guided the big bomber by radar to within fifty meters of the tanker, where Troy took over visually and on-loaded twenty thousand pounds of JP-4.

"Why the hell are we in a radio silent mode?" Candee asked following the refueling. "I thought we were supposed to make lots of noise so the Soviets would turn on their electronic gear. Did I miss something?"

"Guess this is the day we're supposed to surprise 'em," Troy answered.

"In five minutes, we'll be over Saint Lawrence Island," Carl said. "Then we'll turn to a southwesterly heading over the Gulf of Anadyr. From that point on, guys, we'll be within what the Soviets claim as their airspace."

"Okay, crew, listen up," Troy commanded. "Bill, turn around and get those twenty-millimeters warmed up. Let's check our safety and survival gear and tighten our helmets and oxygen masks. We'll be in Indian Country for the next couple of hours.

"Carl, I need you to start calling out distances and times to key checkpoints as well as ETAs to the next turning point. And Bill, I'm already hearing Soviet early-warning radars tracking us. Guess we didn't surprise 'em after all."

"We're eighty miles from Chukotskiy Point," Carl announced. "Our next turn-point will be Navarin in thirty-five minutes."

Candee glanced over his shoulder. "We've pretty much announced our own arrival. We're leaving a stream of puffy white contrails for the world to see. They don't need radar to track us today. I feel like a damn fish in a bowl."

"We're almost over Navarin Point," Carl announced. "For the next forty-five minutes we'll be twenty to thirty miles east of the Soviet coastline."

"Hey, Troy, can you see the sun reflecting off those silver specks low at three o'clock?" Candee said.

"Yeah, I've been watching 'em, too, Bill."

"I can make out a flight of four. They're still at three o'clock and about fifteen thousand feet below us. Looks to me like they're having trouble getting to our altitude."

"Keep your eye on 'em, Bill. I'm still hearing some EW and intercept radars. As long as they keep searching, we don't have a problem. I just don't want to hear that scary lock-on tone."

"We've penetrated the Soviet coastline," Carl said. "We'll be over their landmass for the next five minutes until we reach Olyutorskiy Point. Then we're back over international airspace for the next fifty minutes."

"Hey, we've lost our playmates," Candee said. "Think they started too late—couldn't make it to our altitude."

"I'm hearing just about every type of Soviet radar I've ever been exposed to in training, and some new stuff, as well," Troy said. "It's got to be a red-letter day for our prepositioned ELINT boys out there. Hope they're getting all this stuff recorded. SAC's sure gonna be happy with results from this mission. It's what this whole Shark Bite operation's about.

"If the Soviets are planning anything, it's got to come at our next turn over Kamchatskiy Point."

"I agree, Troy," Carl said. "We're twenty-eight minutes out. Right now the closest Soviet landmass is seventy-eight miles to our right."

"Bill, when we get near Kamchatskiy Point, let's

keep a close eye out for SAMs," Troy said. "I'm pretty sure I heard a signal from one a few minutes ago."

"Hey, crew, we got company," Candee announced. "A flight of four snuck up at our five o'clock. They're about fifteen miles behind us."

"Bill, turn around and give 'em a couple of warning shots with your twenties," Troy said. "I want 'em to know we see them—and it just might keep 'em from closing. If they get any closer, we're out of here per our rules of engagement. Can you tell what kind of MiGs they are?"

"Not at this distance, Troy. I'm guessing they're 19s or 21s."

The big bomber shuddered as Candee hosed off some short bursts from the twenty-millimeters.

"They don't seem to be closing," Candee said.

"I just heard a search radar from a SAM site," Troy said. "It's that unmistakable, high-pitched *chirp, chirp, chirp*. Keep your eyes open, Bill. Carl, how far are we from Kamchatskiy Point?"

"Three minutes out. When we're over it, we'll turn to 060 and head home."

"The MiGs broke off. Guess they're returning to base. I'm turning my seat back around, Troy, okay?" Candee asked.

"Roger, Bill. And keep your ears tuned for a SAM lock-on. I can hear a whole bunch of SAM search signals. If we're going to get a lock-on and launch, it'll come in the next few minutes. I'll bet that's why the MiGs broke off. They didn't want to get tangled up with their own SAMs."

Suddenly, a steady, high-frequency squealing sent shivers up and down Troy's spine.

"They're locked on! They're locked on!" Candee shouted. "It's a launch! It's coming up at two o'clock."

"I'm holding till the last second," Troy said. "Then I'll break hard left and dive."

"Breaking *now!*"

"Great maneuver, Troy!" Candee exclaimed. "That was a true Enloe break."

The missile exploded harmlessly about five hundred meters high and to their right.

"Okay, guys, let's go home. Carl, give me a heading."

"Holy crap!" Candee shouted. "There's another one at four o'clock! Break hard left — *now!*"

As Troy muscled the bomber into a steep-diving left bank, he turned head-on into yet another SAM trailing a stream of white smoke and coming up at his eight o'clock position. Almost as soon as he spotted it, the missile exploded into a huge ball of yellow-and-red flames thirty meters to their left and below the aircraft, sending chunks of molten metal and shrapnel into the left wing and bottom fuselage. In the crew compartment, it felt like someone had swung a giant bat in midair, landing it squarely on the airplane.

Glancing to the left, Troy saw that a quarter of the left wing and number one engine had been sheared off, leaving behind a jagged stub with shards of hanging metal and fuel pouring out of it. With Candee's help, Troy was able to level the badly wounded bomber long enough to transmit a distress call.

Breaking radio silence and broadcasting on HF and UHF emergency channels, Troy cried out, "Shark Zero-one, *Mayday! Mayday! Mayday!* SAM hit. Shark Zero-one."

With that, Troy turned on the emergency alarm bell and commanded, "Bail out! Bail out! Bail out!"

What remained of the big bomber began a flat spiral to the left.

The aisle floor of the crew compartment had turned into a smoldering cauldron, as flames licked up the wall toward the amplifier racks. Troy felt the bomb-nav hatch and ejection seat explode from the airplane. A second later the pilots' canopy blew off, indicating that Candee had initiated his ejection sequence. Confident that his bomb-nav and copilot had ejected, Troy pulled his visor down, squeezed the triggers, and yanked up on the yellow and black striped handles of his own ejection seat.

The next thing he remembered was looking up at his parachute canopy. He knew he was below fourteen thousand feet because that was the altitude at which the parachute automatically opened. Looking around, Troy was relieved to see two deployed chutes below him. He also spotted the Soviet coastline in the distance.

Realizing he was going to land in the ocean, he reached down to pull the lanyard that released his yellow, one-man lifeboat. A sharp pain darted through his left shoulder—his left arm hung limp and bleeding. By using his right arm, Troy managed to pull the cord on his survival pack. He braced for the inevitable plunge into the choppy and freezing ocean.

Chapter XVI

WITH FORTY POUNDS OF survival gear strapped to his body, Troy hit the water hard. He had forgotten to inflate his life vest and sank to what seemed like the bottom of a black, icy ocean. He found himself in darkness, unable to distinguish which way was up or down.

Spotting a faint halo of light, he fought his way toward it, choking from gulps of seawater. His eardrums and lungs were ready to explode as they screamed for air. Finally breaking through the surface, he became entangled in his parachute lines as wet nylon panels slapped at his face. With his one good arm, he struggled to free himself and after several failed attempts was able to drag his exhausted body into the one-man liferaft.

Exhausted and shivering violently, Troy mumbled to himself over and over again, *God help me, God help me.* As he tried to catch his breath and regain some strength, he cautioned himself not to panic; above all he needed to keep his head about him. He felt lucky to be alive. Concern for his fellow crewmen soon gnawed at his mind. Where were they? He tried to look about his surroundings, but the water was choppy and towering waves pushed and shoved him. He couldn't see farther than a few feet.

Pulling out his dripping survival radio, Troy keyed the transmit button, fearful it wouldn't work. "*Mayday, Mayday*. This is Shark Zero-one, Alpha."

Relief washed over him as he heard a response. "Roger, Shark Zero-one, this is Larkspur. What is your condition?" Larkspur was a prepositioned ELINT aircraft orbiting sixty miles offshore.

"Larkspur, I'm in my raft. My left arm and shoulder are injured."

"Roger, Zero-one, alpha. Hang on, we're organizing a rescue."

Suddenly, a small, wooden fishing boat cut its motor, as Troy watched in surprise as it pulled alongside his dinghy. Two husky deck hands reached down and hoisted him onboard, along with his survival gear and raft. It was obvious the Russian boat captain thought he was rescuing a Soviet flier. At first he seemed confused but friendly, even after he realized he had taken aboard a foreigner—an American.

Troy was hustled below deck and handed a hot cup of what tasted like bland potato soup. His equipment and radio were confiscated. When the captain noticed that Troy's shoulder and arm were injured, he ordered his reluctant wife to fashion a makeshift sling from a tablecloth to hold his shoulder in place.

The captain, a grandfatherly and kindly-looking man with bushy white hair and a weathered face, spoke some English. He informed Troy that there had been a time in an earlier war when Americans and Russians were friends and allies. The captain's wife interrupted their conversation, and Troy watched as a heated discussion ensued. The woman reached to turn on the ship's radio, but the captain jerked her hand away.

The captain looked toward Troy, annoyed. "Old woman think trouble with government if I no give you to Soviets," he explained.

Troy laid his hand on the old captain's shoulder and met his watery blue eyes. "Thank you."

It seemed to Troy that the old man had been saving up for years to practice his English, which was badly flawed but understandable. In nonstop broken English phrases, the captain explained how, years ago, he had befriended an American named Eddie Brodski from Philadelphia. They had worked together as mechanics on lend-lease airplanes that the Americans flew to Russia to bolster Russia's air power in its fight against the Nazis. He had learned English from Brodski and had taught Brodski some Russian. The captain told Troy that the two men still exchanged Christmas cards.

Troy begged the old man to let him use his hand-held radio. "I need to let someone know I'm alive."

The old fisherman shook his head sadly. "It is too dangerous. The Soviets—they will be listening."

Just then a huge wave nearly lifted the small craft out of the water. Cupboards tumbled open, and pots and pans crashed to the floor. The captain flew up the ladder to the deck.

As Troy peered through an opening in the deck, he saw that a large, motorized Soviet patrol boat had pulled alongside the fishing craft. The Soviet captain was shouting through a megaphone. He suspected that the Soviets were scouring the area for his crew.

The two captains exchanged harsh words in a back-and-forth shouting match. Then, in spite of the old fisherman's protests, four uniformed, armed sailors boarded the small craft and shoved the captain hard against the cabin bulkhead on their way to below deck. Confronting Troy, they pushed him to the floor and tied his wrists behind his back, further aggravating his painful shoulder. They jerked him backwards up the ladder, placed him in a makeshift, wire fishing basket, and hoisted him aboard the Soviet vessel.

Before being hustled below deck, Troy noticed a deflated yellow dinghy and a tangled parachute piled in a corner of the Soviet vessel. As he tried to get a better look, a guard punched him in the small of the back with the butt of a rifle—but Troy's spirits soared. Maybe Carl and Bill had been rescued and were on the boat!

·····

At SAC headquarters, General Strong was notified of the shoot-down by his aide, Colonel Bill Murphy. When he heard that it was Captain Troy Bench and crew, the general exhaled heavily. "Damn, that boy sure knows how to stay in the thick of things. Hope he's got nine lives—he may need every one of 'em. Bill, let me know when the families have been officially notified. I want to call each one personally."

·····

Within an hour of the shoot-down, the secretary of defense and the chairman of the Joint Chiefs of Staff crossed the Potomac and briefed the president. So far, the Soviets had made no mention of the incident, nor had the media gotten wind of it—but it was only a matter of time.

"The Soviets are just waiting for the right moment to maximize the propaganda value," the president said. "By the way, how far out to sea was the plane when it was hit?"

"Thirteen miles, sir," the secretary of defense replied.

"What the hell were they doing that close? Who

gave 'em permission to be that damned close?" The president looked closely at the secretary. "Get me a detailed briefing on this right away," he ordered.

....

Wendy answered the doorbell and was surprised to see five Air Force officers in dress blues standing at the door. Colonel Blauw and Mark Denman were in front.

"Wendy, may we come in?" Colonel Blauw asked.

Wendy didn't move as her surprise quickly turned into icy fear. Her heart raced as she asked in a low, husky voice, "Is Troy alive?"

"Yes, Wendy, he is," Colonel Blauw said.

She closed her eyes and allowed herself a small moment of relief. "What has happened?" she asked.

"Wendy, may we come in?"

"Yes, yes, come in."

Colonel Blauw quickly introduced the notification team, which included a chaplain along with personnel and finance officers.

Wendy nodded impatiently. "What has happened?" she demanded.

Blauw explained that SAC headquarters had notified them that Troy was missing following an aircraft incident. He had ejected from his bomber at sea. "We know he's alive. An aircraft in the vicinity received a short radio message from him saying that he had an injured shoulder and arm but was otherwise okay."

"Then why hasn't he been rescued?" Wendy asked in confusion.

"I'm sorry, but we have no other information. I promise to provide you with any new developments as we get them," Colonel Blauw said.

The finance officer started to explain that Troy's pay and benefits would continue as usual. Wendy coldly cut him short. "I'm sorry, Captain. I'm not the least bit interested in that right now."

Mark gently took Wendy by the arm and asked whether she would like him to stay. "No ... no, Mark, but thanks. I think I'd just like to be alone right now."

After the group departed, Wendy tearfully dialed her mother in Anaheim. "Mom, I need you. Can you please come over? I need you *now!*"

....

Military officials were repeating the same next-of-kin notification protocol at Dyess AFB, Texas, with Linda Olson, Carl's wife, and at Lubbock, Texas, with Bill Candee's parents.

The Air Force had officially classified the three airmen as *missing*.

Chapter XVII

THE SOVIET GUARDS DUMPED Troy onto the floor of a small storage room in the hold of the patrol boat and slammed the hatch shut, cloaking him in impenetrable darkness. He guessed his captors were the Soviet equivalent of the Coast Guard. The pain in his arm and shoulder had intensified, and spasms shot down his spine to the bottom of his left foot. Making things worse, the putrid smell of rotting fish in his new confinement area made his stomach spasm with nausea.

But he was alive. He said a prayer, thanking God for sparing his life and asking that He watch over Wendy and their unborn child.

After what seemed like hours of bouncing around in turbulent seas, the boat docked, the hatch opened, and light streamed in, temporarily blinding Troy. Two hefty Soviet sailors reached down and grabbed him by his tethered wrists, hoisting him roughly onto the deck. He screamed in agony as unrelenting pain pierced through his body. He steeled himself to stay conscious.

Blindfolded, Troy sensed that he was being placed in the back of a vehicle. As he waited, he leaned back against the seat to relieve his pain and found that he could see through a slit in the bottom of his blind-fold.

What he saw took his breath away. Two sailors carried a stretcher down the wooden gangplank of the vessel, bearing a body wrapped in a soiled white sheet except for one partially exposed foot. Troy's heart sank in despair. He watched as the men placed the stretcher haphazardly among grain sacks in the bed of a military vehicle that quickly drove away. Could the body be Carl or Candee? Just then the guard glanced toward Troy and became aware that he could see from under the blindfold. Shouting angrily in Russian, the guard yanked the blindfold tighter. Once again Troy was in darkness.

After a jarring five-hour drive over potholed roads, someone removed the blindfold and wrist ties and led Troy out of the vehicle and into a gray stone building that appeared to be some sort of military headquar-ters. He recognized the name on the upper parapet of the building: Petropavlovsk, the largest city on the Kamchatka Peninsula and home base for a major So-viet naval facility. Ushered into a drab, windowless room, Troy found himself seated across a table from a smiling Soviet officer with dark, piercing eyes and thick eyebrows, who introduced himself as Lieutenant Colonel Sergei Sevinski of the Soviet Air Force.

"Captain Troy Bench, we know all about you. We know that you were flying a Strategic Air Command B-47 bomber. We know that you were selected to captain this airplane because you had become somewhat of a folk hero by saving the life of a fellow airman. You see, Captain Bench, you should not try to deceive us. I, too, graduated from an American high school in Washington, D.C. My father was in the Washington diplomatic corps, so I know your American ways."

Troy was not surprised to hear that the Soviets knew who he was; the Soviet boat captain had removed Troy's dog tags when he was taken aboard. Shark crews were ordered to carry minimal personal ID on penetration missions: dog tags with name, rank, serial number, and blood type; a Geneva Conventions card; and a cloth blood chit, a small instrument that offered a reward for the bearer's repatriation. Crew members had to leave wallets, rings, ID cards, and other personal items at Eielson for safekeeping.

Moving in closer to Troy, and with a cigarette dangling from his chafed lips, the colonel asked, "Tell me, Captain Bench, why did you violate Soviet airspace?"

Weary, hungry, and in severe pain, Troy searched his mind to recall the dos and don'ts of interrogations that he'd been taught in Air Force Survival School. He remembered being instructed to speak slowly and delay his answers as long as possible. Doing so would give him more time to develop an appropriate response and was also apt to frustrate the interrogator and place him on the defensive.

"My name is Captain Troy Bench, and my serial number is 45—"

"Captain Bench," the colonel interrupted, "you are a smart man, and I am a smart man, so let's stop this charade. We should be able to discuss this in a calm, intelligent manner."

"Okay, Colonel, let's do that. Where is my crew? I demand to see them. And I need a doctor to treat my shoulder."

"All in good time, Captain Bench. You must first answer my questions." The colonel leaned back in his chair and regarded Troy with a thoughtful expression. "We know you took off from Alaska. Your navigation cannot be so faulty, Captain Bench, that you would end up over the Soviet Union by mistake. We could have stopped you earlier with our MiG fighters, but we acted humanely; we hoped you would turn away. But when you continued into our airspace, we were forced to shoot you down with our missiles. Now, Captain Bench, you are in big trouble."

Troy regarded the colonel in silence.

"I ask you," the colonel said, "what is the mission

of Shark crews? You see, we also know the code name for your mission."

"Colonel, I demand to know the status of my crew. Where are they? What is their physical condition? You will get nothing from me until *you* have answered *my* questions. And Colonel, you know that the Geneva Conventions call for immediate release of that information."

"Do not attempt to lecture me on *your* rights, Captain," Colonel Sevinski's fist crashed down hard on the small wooden table as his gentle façade crumbled. His face reddened, and beads of sweat appeared on his forehead. Troy could see that the colonel's fist was paining him.

"You will sit here and think about what I have asked, and be prepared to answer *my* questions upon my return," the colonel said, his voice raising. "If not, you will face the consequences, and they will not be pretty, Captain Bench."

Colonel Sevinski walked briskly out of the room, leaving Troy to his thoughts. Overwhelmed with fatigue, Troy folded his arms on the table, rested his head on them, and fell into a fitful slumber.

....

General Strong, SAC's commander in chief, and Colonel Jack Sparks flew from their Omaha headquarters to Washington to brief the secretary of defense and the president.

"Mr. President," said General Strong, "the electronic intelligence gleaned from this mission is significant. Captain Bench and his crew brought the Soviet air defense systems to life—they went wild. We captured more electronic intelligence on this mission than we've recorded in years. The bomber-crew-turned-reconnaissance-crew ruse succeeded beyond all expectations!"

"Okay, I'm glad everything worked for us," the president said, "but I want the Shark operation to stand down for now. An hour ago, our chargé d'affaires in Moscow was handed a letter of protest, charging us with violating Soviet airspace. They made no mention of the disposition of Captain Bench and his crew. We've filed a letter of protest demanding the crew's immediate return."

"Mr. President, I should explain something at this point," said General Strong. "The reason we chose young crews for the Shark Bite missions was that if a situation such as this arose, we could employ a cover story that the crew was young and inexperienced and accidentally strayed off course. But, Mr. President, in view of the extraordinary success of Bench and his crew, I do not feel we should diminish their courage and skill by masking the event in this kind of cover story."

"I agree, General, we won't do that. But I'll tell you right now, when *The Washington Post* or the *Times* gets a hold of this thing, there's no telling how they'll skew it. They may go positive, or they could head in a negative direction on us."

Glancing toward his secretary of state, the president continued. "George, I want state to handle this, and let's get out in front on it. Call in the leading half-dozen newspaper editors, and give them a heads-up. Be straightforward and honest with them. Hopefully, it'll pay off. And George, keep DOD informed of everything you do."

Walking toward the Oval Office windows, the president regarded the activities on Pennsylvania Avenue. "Gentlemen, this is damn sensitive stuff. We cannot afford to screw it up." He turned back toward the group with urgency. "I want those boys back on American soil ASAP."

"Everyone understand the international impact of this thing?" The president looked in the face of each of his key players. There were nods all around.

"Well, then, let's get moving."

....

The president didn't have long to wait. Within twenty-four hours the Kremlin issued the following announcement: "A United States jet bomber has barbarically intruded into Soviet airspace. However, our heroic Soviet military forces were able to shoot down the intruder and capture two of the crewmen; one died in the shoot-down. The body has been recovered. The surviving intruders are now being detained in Moscow. At the appropriate time, they will be brought to trial as war criminals."

A note with the names of the downed airmen was handed to the American ambassador in Moscow: Captain Troy A. Bench and First Lieutenant Carl V. Olson. First Lieutenant William S. Candee was killed in the shoot-down. The note also contained a stern warning that "this type of aggressive behavior" would not be tolerated. The American ambassador demanded to meet with the airmen, but the Kremlin denied his request.

Over the next few days, the incident made front-page headlines and was the prime topic of discussion on the radio and television.

Amid the flurry of news reports, the president summoned the Soviet ambassador to the White House. "Mr. Ambassador, I demand that you allow our ambassador to meet with our airmen. And I expect you to show humanitarian resolve for our deceased airman and allow for the immediate return of Lieutenant Candee's body to American soil.

"And, Mr. Ambassador, I want you to pass on to the premier that if one hair on the head of either of these airmen is disturbed, I will hold him personally responsible." He shook his finger at the Soviet ambassador. "You make that crystal clear to the premier. And I expect your people to provide all necessary medical care to Captain Bench and Lieutenant Olson.

"Do you understand me? Do I make myself perfectly clear, Mr. Ambassador?"

"Yes, Mr. President, I do understand and I will relay your exact words to the premier," the ambassador said. "But, Mr. President, *you* must understand that these airmen violated our peaceful airspace. They shall have to face trial for that intrusion."

"Mr. Ambassador, do you play poker?"

"On occasion, Mr. President."

"Do you understand the term 'ace in the hole'?"

"Yes, Mr. President, I do."

"Then, let's say that the Soviet Union and the United States are playing poker. The Soviet Union has one ace in the hole, and the United States of America has three. Mr. Ambassador, if the USSR wants to play poker with me, they're going to lose big-time. You see, I have lots of aces in the hole. You tell that to your premier, Mr. Ambassador, and you tell him that I *will use* these aces unless he reconsiders his ploy of putting these young airmen on public trial."

Moving closer, the president looked the ambassador in the eye. "Mr. Ambassador, I want these young men returned immediately to American control. Understand?"

"I will relay every word, Mr. President."

The president pressed the button on his desk intercom marked "secretary."

"Dorothy, get me some background on these officers, and then get their next-of-kin on the phone. I want to talk to each of them personally."

"Yes, Mr. President."

Chapter XVIII

I<small>N THE BOWELS OF</small> the infamous Lubyanka prison in the center of Moscow, the Soviet KGB subjected Troy to brutal interrogations.

Air Force Survival School had trained Troy in techniques for resisting the physical and psychological stresses of interrogations. But after days of questioning in Petropavlovsk; an exhausting five-thousand-mile journey by train, truck, and airplane across Russia to Moscow; and the sapping of his strength from the wounds he suffered during the shoot-down and capture, Troy was sure he was easy prey for the well-prepared KGB agents in Moscow. Sharp pain numbed his body and mind. His left arm hung limp at his side, and his tattered flight suit still bore evidence of dark, clotted bloodstains from the shoot-down.

Three metal folding chairs and a wooden table with heavy spindled legs were the only furniture in the drab interrogation room. A frayed electric cord with a porcelain socket and a clear glass bulb dangled from the ceiling, separating Troy from his interrogators. The bulb pulsated in sync with Moscow's power surges.

The KGB agents preyed on Troy's vulnerabilities. Pacing back and forth, they recited his personal history, leading him to believe that they knew much more than they actually did.

"We know you were born in Bisbee, America. We know you graduated in first class at new air academy in Colorado. We know your wife's name is Wendy and that she is with child."

Troy's stomach wrenched. *How did they get this information so quickly?*

Applying age-old interrogation techniques, one agent promised medical attention and food, while the other threatened continued physical and psychological abuse.

"Tell us, Captain Bench," the robust chief interrogator shouted, "why did you violate Soviet airspace? What secret electronic black boxes did you have onboard?"

"I am an American military officer. My serial number is …"

Troy recoiled off the wall from a body blow to his left shoulder. Tears stung his eyes, and he screamed in pain as he crumpled to the floor. He wondered how much longer he could resist. He knew he was at the outer limits of his physical and mental endurance.

Lifted by two hefty guards, he was dragged by his arms down a dark, narrow passageway to an eight-by-eight-foot cell and dumped on the floor. The massive iron door slammed shut, and to Troy it felt like the final nail in his coffin. Too weak to climb onto his cot, and overwhelmed by throbbing pain, Troy succumbed to a restless sleep on the cold concrete floor.

....

The clanging of keys on his cell door awakened Troy with a start. Three uniformed guards, along with a stout woman with a stethoscope hanging from her neck and her hair pulled tightly into a bun, entered the cell.

Viewing Troy laying prostrate and bleeding on the floor, the woman gasped. "My God!" She ordered the guards to lift him carefully and place him on the three-wheeled gurney. The woman, clad in a wrinkled but spotless white medical coat, then introduced herself as Doctor Helga Khrushova.

Bending down, her face close to his, she spoke loudly with a broken English accent,. "Captain Bench, can you hear me?"

"Yes … yes, I can," he mumbled.

"Captain Bench, we have been ordered by the Kremlin to clean you up and give you a complete physical. We will also examine your wounded shoul-

der and arm. You will be under my care for the remainder of the day. I expect full cooperation during
all tests and examinations. So long as you do as I say,
you will be treated well. Do you understand me, Captain Bench?"

"Yes, ma'am, I do." Troy felt like a little boy whose
mother had told him how to behave on his first day
of school.

The guards strapped Troy onto the gurney and
transported him to a room with several shower
heads. The pungent smell of lye burned his nostrils
and made his eyes water.

"Captain Bench, you take shower now." Troy
waited for the doctor to leave the room, but instead
she plopped her beefy body on a three-legged wood-
en stool at the entrance to the shower room. "Why are
you waiting, Captain Bench? Take off your clothes,
and take your shower now," she ordered. "We have
much to do."

For an awkward moment, Troy stood motionless,
but then slowly and painfully took off his clothes and
turned on the spigot. The water was icy cold, but felt
invigorating against his skin and his wounds. The lye
soap was rough, wiry, and reeked of disinfectant, but
after what had taken place over the past several days,
Troy was grateful for the opportunity to get cleaned
up.

"Put these on." The doctor handed him some

oversized, baggy clothes. They were more like pajamas than street clothes, but they were clean. After an orderly X-rayed him from every angle and extracted five tubes of blood, Troy was strapped into a wheelchair and rolled to Doctor Khrushova's office. A Soviet soldier who spoke no English stood guard at the entrance.

The doctor clipped the X-rays onto a viewing screen. "Captain Bench, as you can see, you have a small hairline fracture of your collarbone and a one-centimeter fracture of your upper left arm, as well as many bruises and lacerations that will take some time to heal. As a precaution, I'm putting you in a partial upper-body cast that you will remain in for two weeks. It will keep your body from being further damaged during interrogations."

Troy looked intently into the doctor's face. "What did you just say?"

"I'm sorry, but I dare not repeat it."

"May I ask where you received your medical training, doctor?"

"I received most of it in London during the war. My father was a Russian liaison officer attached to the Royal Air Force. But we shall not talk of this. It is not wise."

Two hours later the cast was in place, and Troy was wheeled back to a different cell, this one a little cleaner and with a thin mattress. He wondered what had prompted his captors' change in attitude.

In the days ahead, the interrogations became more humane. One day a Soviet military officer conducted them, the next day a KGB agent tried to pry mission secrets from him. The doctor was right; the interrogators were reluctant to rough him up now that his upper body was encased in white plaster. They still shouted and shook their fists in his face, but the physical violence diminished.

Troy seemed to be housed alone in an isolated catacomb of the prison. The lack of human contact made him actually look forward to the questioning sessions, now that the physical violence had subsided. At least the sessions gave him a chance to spar mentally with another human being.

At every session, he asked the same questions: "What happened to my crew? Where are they? Are they injured? You'll not get a thing from me until you inform me about the condition of my crew." The interrogators would then withdraw with blank, emotionless stares.

Troy had begun to wonder if it was possible that friendly forces had rescued Carl and Candee. Maybe he was the only one interned. Was it possible that the body he had seen wrapped in a sheet wasn't Bill or Carl? He prayed that that was the case.

Troy had become fond of sparring with one particular Soviet Air Force interrogator, Major Georgi Kuzvetsky, who Troy nicknamed Kuzy. Both men had an amateur interest in world aerobatic competitions and stunt planes. Kuzy had started building an aerobatic airplane several years earlier but had been transferred before the plane could be completed. He explained that it was stored in an old family barn in central Russia and that he intended to finish it some day. Troy empathized with him; it was something he too had dreamed of doing.

Troy asked Kuzy about his crew. "Where are they, and what's their condition?" The major stared at him a long while without speaking, and then got up and left the room. He returned some fifteen minutes later.

"I am prepared to tell you about your crew," Kuzy said, "but in return you must tell me about the nature of your mission and why you penetrated our airspace. I must have something in return, you understand?"

"I agree," Troy said.

Troy had anticipated that this moment might present itself and had concocted a cover story that the Soviets just might believe. He knew that the USSR had been conducting nuclear tests near the Kamchatka Peninsula in violation of United Nations' testing agreements. The United States was concerned that these tests would contaminate the rich Alaskan fishing fields in the northern Pacific. Having had a course in oceanography at the Academy, Troy thought he just might be able to pull it off, at least string them along until he was able to gain some knowledge on the condition of his crew. What did he have to lose?

During questioning by his Soviet interrogators, he parceled out tidbits of knowledge until they offered up new information based on his responses. At least for the moment it seemed to work.

"We will verify what you have told us, Captain Bench. If you have lied to us, you will suffer."

Major Kuzvetsky returned to the room. His face was solemn. "I regret to inform you, Captain Bench, that Lieutenant William S. Candee was killed either during the shoot-down or during his ocean landing. His body was recovered at sea entangled in his parachute. His body has been turned over to the American ambassador."

Troy buried his head in his hands and squeezed so hard it hurt. Tears filled his eyes. Though he always knew this was a possibility, it still came as a shock. Raising his head slowly and fearing the worst, he asked, "And Carl Olson? What about Lieutenant Olson?"

"Lieutenant Olson was picked up by a fishing trawler. He is unharmed except for minor wounds and is being detained in Moscow."

"I want to see him," Troy demanded.

"It is not possible at this time, Captain Bench."

Troy's cast felt like dead weight encasing his body; his heart was heavy, and he struggled to breathe. "I would like to be returned to my cell," he said in a husky voice.

As soon as his cell door closed, Troy lay on his cot and allowed himself to think about what had taken place. One of his best friends was dead, and he felt responsible. Bill was the crackup on the crew—always full of life. How could he be dead? He was both the cynic and the optimist; he was the "I don't give a shit" guy, and the one who cared. Most of all, he was just a happy-go-lucky Texas cowboy who Troy had been blessed to know. Troy missed him terribly. Tears welled up in his eyes, and he sobbed uncontrollably.

"Damn you people!" Troy shouted through his tears. "Damn this place! It was all my fault."

Could he have done something differently to avert this catastrophe? Had he failed in his mission? Did he somehow miss a SAM warning? Could he have done a better job of evaluating the SAM threat? If he had terminated the mission just seconds earlier, Bill would be alive. And what about an international incident—did he cause one? How was the free world viewing all of this?

Troy thought of Wendy going through her pregnancy alone. And his parents—how were they coping under all of the stress?

Troy agonized for what seemed like hours, but as

his tears subsided, he gradually realized that there wasn't one damn thing he could do about any of it. What he needed to concentrate on was maintaining his stamina. He willed himself to become mentally and physically tougher. After all, he had a wife and a baby on the way to return home to.

For a split second in the quiet of his cell, he thought he could hear Bill Candee shouting at him: *Dammit, Troy! Get a goddamn grip on yourself. You gotta beat these bastards at their own game. You can do it, man, you can outthink 'em—I know you can. Be tough, Troy!*

With a deep breath, Troy renewed his determination *not* to provide the Soviets with any information about his mission. He would employ every technique of evasion that he had learned in survival school. Above all, he would maintain his pride and his integrity. And when released, he would walk out with his head held high. After all, he was an Air Force Academy grad, and that's what he'd been trained to do: fly and fight.

Chapter XIX

INQUISITIVE LOCALS AND A national media circus of news vans, parked nearly in her front yard, had become too much for Wendy. Colonel Blauw and Mark Denman had encouraged her to leave Riverside. Blauw assured her that he would call daily and update her the moment he heard something new on Troy. With Mark's help, she packed a few things and stole away in the middle of the night for her parents' farm near Anaheim. Wendy had always been close to her family, and now that she was in her second trimester, she found even more comfort in being with them.

"Mom, it's hard to believe, but I received calls from the president and from General Strong at Omaha this week. The president assured me that the government was pursuing all diplomatic avenues to obtain Troy's and Carl's release. He also said that the Soviet ambassador had ensured him that both men were in good health and residing in clean, comfortable quarters. I really hope that's true."

Wendy looked at her mother in anguish. "God, Mom, I just miss him terribly, and I worry how he's being treated. I'm so frustrated that I can't do anything but sit here."

"I know, honey. But he'll be home soon—I just know it."

"I feel badly that I haven't called Carl's wife more often," Wendy said as her mother patted her arm in comfort. "I know this is all as painful for Linda as it is for me."

"I'm sure she understands, honey," her mother said. "Doesn't she have two little girls to care for? She's probably pretty busy."

"When we talked last week she said her parents were on their way from Colorado to help out."

Wendy massaged her temples, where the pangs of a headache were just beginning. "Mom, I may be a wimp, but it was all I could do to muster enough strength to attend Bill Candee's memorial service at March last week. Everyone wanted to console me— they were all so thoughtful and giving. But, honestly, all I wanted to do was get out of there. I just don't feel comfortable around a lot of people right now."

"Honey, that's perfectly natural," her mother reassured her.

"Oh, I almost forgot. You remember me talking

about Troy's bomb-nav, Joe Mangino? Well, he called and said he and his wife Gail were on their way over. Joe wants to drop off the personal effects Troy had with him in Alaska."

When Wendy's mother looked confused, Wendy reminded her that Joe had been appointed summary court officer and had to inventory and box up Troy's things.

"That couldn't have been easy for him," her mother murmured sympathetically.

When the Manginos arrived later that day, Wendy asked Joe to stack the boxes in one of her Mom's closets. The last thing she wanted was to go through her husband's belongings.

They sat on the glassed-in porch overlooking her parents' vineyards, quietly sipping a glass of last year's white zinfandel.

Suddenly, Wendy's words rushed forth in a burst of emotion. "Joe, tell me what really happened on that mission and what Shark Bite is all about. I want to know the details—I *need* to know the details. I've heard so many conflicting stories in the past couple of weeks. I don't really know what to believe anymore."

Joe provided as much detail as he dared without getting into classified information, but knew he hadn't come close to satisfying Wendy's curiosity. "Wendy, I'm just sorry I wasn't with the crew that day. I wish

I hadn't been sick. Maybe there's something I could have done. I don't know what ... but I should have been there."

Joe seemed to struggle to get his words out. "I just can't believe Bill Candee's gone ... I'm not—I'm not sure I'll ever be able to accept it. He was so full of life ... and such a good friend. He made us all laugh, Wendy."

Gail reached over and squeezed her husband's hand, her eyes brimmed with emotion and empathy.

Enveloped in her own problems, Wendy hadn't realized how distraught Joe had become with all that had taken place and how guilty he felt for not having been with his crew that fateful day. Although she still had a lot of questions about the mission, she decided not to pressure him any further—for now.

When Joe and Gail got up to leave moments later, she gave Joe a warm hug. "Joe, Troy is so lucky to have you as a friend. Everything's going to work out just fine. He'll be home soon."

Wendy was surprised at the confidence and optimism she had summoned. She suddenly realized how right it was for her to be on the farm and away from the hubbub in Riverside. She could think more clearly, and most importantly, she was with her family.

In his new environment at Lubyanka, Troy found

plenty to annoy him over and above the endless hours of boredom. The overhead light that dangled from the ceiling of his small cell stayed on continuously. At first he found it difficult to sleep under such conditions but adapted somewhat by pulling a blanket over his head. Then there was the guard who walked up and down the dingy hall, every half hour, banging a large metal pipe on the steel bars. Not to mention the food wasn't exactly home cooking. Tasting like fish gruel without the fish, it was shoved into the cell at odd intervals, sometimes every hour or so, and at other times not appearing for twenty-four hours or more. Troy knew that all of these annoyances were part of the Soviet psychological harassment plan; he would just have to be flexible and adapt, and above all, maintain a sense of humor.

During interrogations, he was informed that he would go on public trial in a military court. If found guilty of crimes against the State, he would be banished to a forced labor gulag near the Arctic Circle. His interrogators told him repeatedly that America had forsaken him and his crew and that the United States had denied any knowledge of his flight into Soviet airspace. His interrogators said that the only way Troy could survive and maybe someday be freed was to fully cooperate with them. They went so far as to show him an alleged front page of *The New York Times* with the headline, "Amerika Denys Intruson."

Troy laughed out loud at the misspelled words and awkward font.

The Soviets had gone to a lot of trouble to scare and coerce him, but so far he had been able to withstand the physical and psychological pressures. He wasn't sure how much longer he would be able to keep it up, though. He chuckled when he thought of the Soviet interrogation team member who had thought up *The New York Times* fiasco. This guy surely was in big trouble with his Soviet bosses. Maybe he would even beat Troy to the gulag.

Troy knew better than to believe the Soviet propaganda. He knew America would never abandon its military members. Nevertheless, he had to admit that the daily isolation and mental harassment had begun to take a toll on his mind. He realized that keeping his brain and body fit was more important than ever. One thing that worked for him, and made time go by faster, was designing a virtual home for Wendy—down to the smallest details in the kitchen and bathrooms. He asked for paper and pencil to pursue his ideas but was denied. With nothing to do for long periods of time, he found it comforting to dwell on thoughts of the various stages of his life and his family.

Troy drew strength from reflecting upon his parents' stories about the early days when they were both immigrants in Bisbee. Each day of their young lives in

America brought them problems and hardships that they were forced to confront and overcome.

His father had emigrated from the Slovak region of southern Europe. Upon his arrival in America, he had shortened his name from Stepffen Benchovic to Steven Bench—he wanted to look and sound American. Like most immigrants of that era, Steven Bench wasn't afraid of hard work; he had come to America to earn a better life for himself, and he was prepared to do whatever it took.

Lying on his cot and staring at the ceiling light, Troy remembered his father telling him stories about the fifteen-hour shifts he used to work as a mucker and hard-rock driller in the Copper Queen mine. His father had met Troy's mother, an immigrant from Mexico, at a local dance marathon in Bisbee. Winning the dance contest that night started a lifelong relationship. They were married soon after.

Angelica Antoinette Martinez, or Angie, as his father called her, was employed as a domestic and nanny at the home of a Phelps Dodge mining executive in Bisbee. Aside from a strong physical attraction, his father and mother found commonality in their Catholic faith and in their desire for a family. Early on, they instilled in their children the values of responsibility and hard work. English only was spoken in the home. Troy recalled his father saying in his heavy Slovak accent, "We are Americans now. We will speak English."

....

Troy had not seen daylight for weeks. He wasn't exactly sure how long; for twenty-four hours a day, the only light he saw was the continuously burning ceiling light in his windowless cell and the dangling light bulb over his interrogator's table. He had lost all sense of time and place. With no way of knowing whether it was night or day, and with no outside noises to judge time by, he had lost a sense of life's equilibrium. His lack of sleep worsened his perspective. When he *could* sleep, it came only in short snippets.

During interrogations Troy was ordered to stand for long periods. Although he hadn't received any physical abuse since he had been placed in the cast, the constant strain on his body was excruciating. He slumped to the floor several times during his last interrogation, only to have the Soviet guards jerk him back to a standing position each time.

Days turned into weeks, and he lost hope for an early release. His only positive thought was that the longer he stayed at Lubyanka, the better the odds were that he wouldn't be killed or sent to a gulag.

He had repeatedly asked his captors for paper and pencil to write Wendy a letter. Each time his request was denied unless he would be willing to make a written statement admitting crimes against the people of the USSR—something he was unwilling to do.

Upon returning to his cell after one lengthy and verbally combative session, Troy's emotions erupted. He broke down, sobbing uncontrollably. Not knowing when a day started or ended, or if or when he would be released, had exacted a heavy emotional toll.

Gathering what mental strength he could muster, he resolved to begin a vigorous physical calisthenics regimen in spite of his restrictive cast and the lack of space. He vowed to spend more time on mental exercises as well. He loved geometry—recalling formulas for areas and volumes would surely task his brain. He also looked forward to reliving the wonderful segments of his life with Wendy. It would be like watching a home movie. All of these tasks would help take his mind off himself. He had to get organized, regardless of the difficulty.

Troy demanded a timepiece from his captors, and to his great surprise, his Air Force "hack" watch was returned. Now at last he could restore some semblance of order to his life. Getting his sleep schedule on track he set as a priority.

Troy continued to inquire about Carl during each interrogation—and each time his inquiries were met with blank stares from his captors.

His cast had become troublesome and irritating.

It itched, smelled bad, and interfered with his new exercise program. He felt that whatever healing was supposed to take place had probably run its course, so he asked to see his doctor. Again to his surprise, Doctor Khrushova arrived at his cell the following morning.

"Good morning, Captain Bench. How have you been feeling?"

"Better every day, Doc." Troy felt like he was greeting an old friend, a person who was there to help, not interrogate.

With the doctor were two husky orderlies, non-English speaking, who strapped him into a wheelchair and rolled him through several dimly lit corroders. They rode a creaky elevator that Troy sensed might give way any second.

"First, Captain Bench, we will take X-rays to see how the healing has progressed. If your fractures have healed, we shall remove the cast. Have you had any problems with your injuries or with any health problems?"

"No, ma'am, I've been in fine health—almost ready to launch a prison break." Troy felt comfortable with the doctor, although it was obvious she didn't find his comment amusing.

"Captain Bench, the X-rays show that your collarbone and your arm have healed sufficiently for us to remove the cast. I think you should take a shower once the cast is cut off."

Again, the doctor sat cross-legged on her stool while Troy showered. The burning stench of the lye soap gave Troy confidence that no germ could possibly linger after coming in contact with the disinfectant.

When Troy had finished showering and dressing, he asked, "Doctor, could you tell me when I saw you last?"

Glancing at Troy curiously, the doctor moved her index finger swiftly through his health records to a date. "Four weeks and two days ago, Captain."

Troy was surprised that so much time had elapsed. With the return of his watch, he could now keep track of dates and time. He decided to press his luck further. "Doctor Khrushova, how is my friend, Lieutenant Olson?"

She replied without hesitation, "Lieutenant Olson is now in good health. He has no broken bones. Like you, he has some shrapnel wounds that have healed. I suggest you keep this knowledge to yourself, Captain."

Smiling, Troy reached across the examining table and lightly squeezed her hand. "Thank you, Doctor. Thank you very much for all you've done." She acknowledged the gesture with a slight nod.

Troy's spirits soared as the guards who had waited outside walked him back to his cell. Finally, he had found out that Carl was well and also at Lubyanka. With this knowledge and the absence of the unwieldy cast, he walked with a new spring in his step.

Chapter XX

"Mom, could you get the phone?" Wendy shouted. "I'm still in the shower."

"It's Linda Olson in Abilene. Should I have her call back?"

"No, I'll take it in the bedroom; she might have news from Washington." Wendy quickly wrapped herself in a towel and picked up the phone in the bedroom. "Hi, Linda. Anything new on our husbands?"

"No, I haven't heard anything for a couple of days. The Pentagon said they'd let me know if anything popped up. I *do* have a proposition for you. Even though you're in your third trimester, I think it'd be fun if you and I got to know each other better." Although Wendy and Linda had never met, their husbands graduated in the same class at the Academy. "I can't leave Abilene because of my two little girls, but Carl's 96th Bomb Wing Commander, Colonel Bob Smith, thinks that because of our situation he can arrange for a medevac plane to pick you up at March and drop you off at Dyess. The plane is loaded with medical personnel, so you'd be in safe hands. What do you think?"

"That sounds great, Linda. I'm sure my doctor would approve, and it'll be nice to have a change of scenery."

"Good, I'll get back to you tomorrow with the details. It'll be fun—I can't wait."

<hr />

The C-9 Nightingale made one stop at Davis-Monthan in Tucson before landing at Dyess in Abilene in the afternoon. Linda and Colonel Smith met Wendy at the plane in a blue Air Force staff car. He dropped them off at Linda's on-base quarters on Nebraska Avenue, an austere three-bedroom dwelling in the military housing complex.

"Call me if there's anything you ladies need," the colonel said, jotting down his private number on a card and handing it to Linda.

Linda shook his hand. "Thank you for everything, Colonel, and please pass on my thanks to Mrs. Smith. She's been so very kind and helpful to me these past few weeks."

After reading an extra bedtime story to her girls, two-year-old Sara and four-year-old Megan, Linda kissed them good night and joined Wendy in the living room.

"Finally, time to ourselves," Linda said with a warm smile. "So what did your obstetrician tell you about a drink before bed?"

"He told me one couldn't hurt, and I'm ready for one," Wendy said.

Linda mixed two dry martinis, handing one to Wendy.

Then, settling comfortably on the couch, the women talked about their husbands and the emotional impact of the last several weeks on their lives.

"How did you first hear the news about Troy?" Linda asked.

Wendy recounted how the notification team from March told her the news. "They were all very nice and professional, but I don't remember a whole lot of what they said other than that Troy had made a radio transmission saying he was injured. Hours after the government officially announced the shoot-down, media vans and reporters were camped out on my front yard. There were even protestors marching back and forth with signs calling Troy a warmonger."

Wendy shook her head angrily at the memory. "I know my husband. I know that whatever he was involved in, he believed it was honorable or he wouldn't have been a part of it. You're lucky, Linda, that you live on a military reservation and you were protected from all of that."

"It's hard to believe that people can be so malicious and cruel," Linda said sympathetically. "They have no idea the sacrifices our SAC aircrews and their families make every day."

"You're right, they don't know," Wendy agreed. "During those first hours, I had no idea what Troy's medical condition was. For that matter, I didn't even know if he was alive. It was too much for me to deal with. I had to get away. Fortunately my parents live nearby in Anaheim."

During a thoughtful pause in the conversation, Linda drew a deep breath and said, "Wendy, I have a confession."

Wendy looked at her with curiosity.

"I had a big crush on Troy when he was at the Academy and I was attending Denver University," Linda said. "This was way before you met him. It was when the cadets were stationed at Lowry before they moved into their new facility near Colorado Springs. As a matter of fact, I think it was Troy who introduced me to Carl. Once I met Carl, though, I fell head over heels for him."

"I know what you mean, Linda. It was the same way when Troy and I met. We're so lucky to have found them."

"Or it could be we're just smart." Linda smiled as she refilled her martini glass and looked at Wendy's empty glass questioningly.

"I'd better not," Wendy said, waving her hand. "But you go ahead."

Linda settled back onto the couch, taking a sip of her martini. "So tell me about you and Troy. How did you guys meet, and when did you get married? I want to hear all the romantic stuff."

"I guess you could call it a chance meeting," Wendy said, smiling as she recalled the memory. "I was between my second and third year at Arizona State University and had taken a summer job near Colorado Springs as a youth counselor for troubled teenage girls. Troy was about to start his final year at the Air Force Academy and was involved in the summer training and indoctrination of new cadets. It was a Saturday morning, and I was responsible for a busload of girls headed for Denver to play in a softball tournament. Our bus broke down north of Colorado Springs on Monument Hill.

"Troy was on his way to Denver to hang out with some friends for the weekend. He saw us stranded on the side of the road and stopped to help. Long-story-short, Troy got our bus running—something about the carburetor, I think. Then he insisted on following us to Denver to make sure we arrived safely. I invited him to stay and watch our softball game and join us for lunch at McDonald's—my treat." Wendy laughed and rested her hand on her belly fondly.

"Wow, that *was* a chance meeting. Did you date all summer?" Linda asked.

"Oh, absolutely, I wasn't about to let this cute guy get away. We got together as often as possible—whenever our jobs allowed it. But soon it was August and I had to get back to ASU for my junior year. Troy was able to get off for a long weekend, and he drove me to Tempe. During the trip we realized we were very much in love, and throughout the school year we wrote to each other almost every day and got together as often as we could."

Wendy stopped as Linda suddenly looked toward the girls' bedroom. "Hold on a minute, Wendy, I think one of the girls is up. Don't lose your thought. I'll be right back."

Wendy was impressed with how warm and friendly Linda was. She was a natural blonde, about five-five, with boundless energy and the slim, contoured body of a model—even after two kids.

I like Linda, and I'm glad I'm here, Wendy thought. *It makes the loneliness and worry easier to take when it's shared.*

"It was Sara," Linda said, returning to the living room. "She just wanted me to hold her. She really misses her daddy."

"You know what, Linda? I didn't even hear Sara cry."

"You will once you get one of your own. Then

you'll hear even the slightest whimper. But go on with your story—I'm anxious to hear about the rest of the year and the wedding and all that."

"Well, during the next few months we met each other's families. Troy had a couple of days off at Thanksgiving, so we drove to Bisbee. I met his mom, Angie, and his dad, Steven, and his sisters. We all got along so well.

"At Christmas we joined my parents skiing in Vail, Colorado. It was there, while we were walking through Vail one evening, that Troy proposed—and of course I accepted.

"Then we really got lucky. Troy was assigned to a pilot-training class at Williams Air Force Base near Phoenix. It couldn't have worked out better! I attended college at Arizona State in Tempe while he learned to fly jets at nearby Williams Field."

"Did you get married at the Academy chapel like Carl and I did?"

Wendy nodded. "Both our parents wanted us to have a big wedding in either Bisbee or Anaheim, but we wanted to keep it small. The day after Troy's graduation, we got married in the Academy chapel. His family and a couple dozen of our close friends were there. My dad had pneumonia so my parents couldn't come, but they had a reception for us later at their farm in Anaheim."

"Carl and I got married just hours after you did!"

Linda exclaimed. "You know how the first few days after graduation the Academy chapel operates like an assembly line—cranking out weddings, one after another? Well, we got married in the chapel *three* days after graduation. We hosted a reception for about thirty people at the Officers' Club. Mom and Dad and Carl's parents were there. It was the most wonderful day of my life. I think of it often—particularly now that Carl's not here."

Linda sighed, brushing the tears from her eyes and standing up from the couch. "Well, we've got all day tomorrow to talk. You've got to be worn out from flying and all. Let's go to bed."

A knock on the guest-room door woke Wendy from a deep sleep. It was still dark as she glanced at the clock on the nightstand in confusion: 6:10 AM.

"Wendy, are you awake?" She heard Linda's voice through the door. "Your mom's on the phone. You can take it on the kitchen phone."

"Thanks, I'll be right there."

Not even stopping to put on a robe, Wendy ran down the hallway, almost stumbling headlong over a doll house as her mind raced with anxious thoughts. Linda was in the kitchen making coffee.

"Mom, what's up? Is Dad okay?"

"I'm sorry to get you up this early, honey, but Troy's mom has been trying to reach you. His dad had a heart attack last evening in Bisbee. The ambulance took him to the Tucson Medical Center where he underwent surgery. Angie told me he was out of surgery and stable. She asked me to have you call her in Tucson." Wendy reached for a nearby pen and paper and scrawled down a phone number from her mother. "Honey, if there's anything Dad and I can do, please let us know."

"I will, Mom, and thanks for calling. I'll get back to you when I know more. I love you. Bye."

Wendy quickly brought Linda up to date and then waded through the bureaucracy of the Tucson Medical Center telephone system. Finally, she made contact with Troy's mother, Angie. "Steven is still in critical condition in ICU," Angie said, "but his first words after coming out of surgery were, 'I've got to talk to Wendy. It's urgent.' He wouldn't tell me what he wanted to talk with you about. Wendy, I know you've got an awful lot going on in your life now, but I told Steven I would give you his message."

"Angie, I'll make every effort to stop in Tucson on my way back to California. Let me see what I can work out, and I'll get back to you."

Linda seemed to sense the urgency in Wendy's voice. "I'm going to call Colonel Smith and see if he can help get you to Tucson," she said after Wendy hung up the phone. "Why don't you grab a shower before the girls wake up? In the meantime, I'll go to work on your problem and get some breakfast ready for us."

Wendy walked around the counter and gave Linda a grateful hug. "Thanks, Linda ... for everything."

"Hey, remember, we're in this together."

After showering, Wendy walked back into the kitchen to find that Linda had worked out a travel plan for her. "It's all set, Wendy. Colonel Smith arranged for a medevac to come through Dyess this afternoon. He also scheduled a fuel stop at Davis-Monthan, and *you* have a reserved seat. The Davis-Monthan stopover should give you enough time to race to the hospital for a short visit and then fly on to March."

Before boarding the C-9 at Dyess, Wendy gave Linda a warm, encompassing hug and thanked her for a wonderful thirty-hour respite. She next turned to the wing commander. "Colonel, I'm going to throw military protocol out the window and give you a big hug. We," she said, patting her tummy, "can't thank you enough for all you've done."

"It's been *my* privilege to help both of you ladies, and I pray that your husbands will be released soon," the colonel said kindly. "Oh, and one last thing, Mrs. Bench. Lieutenant Sandra Kelly, the Davis-Monthan protocol officer, will meet you at the airplane. She'll drive you to the hospital, and take you back to the base when you've completed your visit."

Wendy's eyes clouded with tears. She was overwhelmed by the kindness of near strangers—who had now become friends.

....

Lieutenant Sandra Kelly, a striking young woman in her fitted, blue Air Force uniform, met the airplane in her personal vehicle, a red Corvette with white bucket seats. As Sandra steered her Vette up Craycroft Road through rush-hour traffic, Wendy discovered that they had a lot in common. They shared experiences owning Corvettes, growing up in Southern California, and playing college softball—Sandra for USC, and Wendy for ASU.

After they pulled up to the hospital, Wendy found Angie waiting in the lobby. They embraced in silence. As they embarked on the long walk down the corridor to ICU, Angie gave Wendy the details of Steven's medical condition. She also warned her not to be alarmed when she saw him.

"I'm so glad you could make the stopover in Tucson, Wendy. I know it was an extra burden at a very difficult time, but Steven's been asking for you since he came out of the anesthesia. It seems he's learned something he can't wait to tell you. You're a very special person in his life, you know."

Although forewarned, Wendy was shocked to see the myriad tubes and oxygen hoses running in and out of Steven's body. Pale and gaunt, he was the shell of the robust man Wendy knew.

Maneuvering her head through the tangle of life-supporting lines, she kissed his forehead. "Papa, are you awake?"

Steven didn't speak, but when he opened his eyes they twinkled and he raised his hand slowly and touched Wendy's face. He slid the plastic oxygen mask down to his chin and hesitantly spoke. "I'm fine now that you're here."

Although his voice was weak and his words slurred, Wendy was thrilled to hear them. "Papa, what is it you want to tell me?"

Speaking slowly and enunciating each word, he began. "I talked with Troy. He said to tell you he's okay … and not to worry. He was tortured at first, but now his interrogations are more humane. He's worried about you and the baby."

He paused, swallowing hard as tears rolled down his cheeks. "Troy said if he isn't back by the time the baby is born, you should name the baby Jack or Megan." He swallowed again. "He said you'd understand."

Dumbfounded, Wendy lifted her head slowly, her eyes moist. Only she and Troy had known about the names; no one else could have possibly known.

Wendy, lowering her head again near Steven's ear, "Papa, when did you have this talk with Troy?" But it was too late; Steven had already dozed off. Wendy gently replaced the oxygen mask and turned to hug Angie, sobbing.

On the way down the long corridor to the waiting room, the two women held each other tightly. "Wendy, there are many things we children of God do not fully understand but must accept," Angie said. "We must be thankful that God found a conduit to convey to us that Troy is okay. We need to accept it without questioning how or why."

In the lobby, Angie and Wendy said their tearful good-byes and Angie promised to keep Wendy appraised of Steven's recovery.

During the drive back to Davis-Monthan, Lieutenant Kelly, sensing that something unusual and traumatic had taken place at the hospital, responded with respectful silence.

Three ambulatory patients had boarded the medevac, and the plane's twin-jet engines were already turning when Lieutenant Kelly drove up to the airplane.

"Thank you so much for everything, Sandra. You'll never know how grateful I am."

"The pleasure is mine, Mrs. Bench. We all pray that Captain Bench and Lieutenant Olson are released soon." With a snappy courtesy salute, Lieutenant Kelly slipped back into her Corvette and drove away.

During the forty-minute flight to March, Wendy

took stock of all that had transpired in the last thirty-six hours. She began to realize that the Air Force, and maybe many Americans, had somehow attached a celebrity status to her and Linda. Although it made her uncomfortable, there wasn't a thing she could do to change it; she would just learn to deal with it.

Chapter XXI

IN HIS MORNING CABINET meeting, the president queried the secretaries of state and defense on their progress for obtaining the release of Captain Bench and Lieutenant Olson. Turning to his secretary of state, he said, "George, I put you in charge of this thing, and I promised the wives of these young airmen that their husbands would be home soon. It's now going on seven weeks. What's the holdup? I want a comprehensive briefing this afternoon, and it better be positive or some heads are gonna roll."

Sergei Orlovsky was a Soviet spy in the early 1960s until the CIA trapped him with a suitcase full of drawings and technical data on America's latest medium-range ballistic missiles. He had coerced a Hughes Missile Company subcontractor into providing top-secret data to be smuggled to the Soviet Union. The subcontractor had been upset with what he perceived as an unfair contract and needed money to stay afloat.

The Soviets wanted Orlovsky returned. Anthony Roget, the CIA director, was first to propose the swap, but at the time the State Department was less than enthusiastic and suggested alternatives. Following unsuccessful overtures to the Soviets concerning the fliers, the State Department became more receptive. Finally, with no other viable options, the secretary of state agreed with the CIA that the Orlovsky swap was worth pursuing.

The CIA and State presented the proposal to the president. The president asked his CIA director whether he thought they were offering too much. "If this thing works and Orlovsky is returned to the Soviets, what assurance do we have that he's not taking a head full of top-secret data back with him?"

Roget assured the president that Orlovsky was not technically oriented; he could not have absorbed the treasure trove of data that he had planned to smuggle.

"If that's true," the president asked, then why are the Soviets so damned eager to get him back?"

"His value to them is twofold, Mr. President. First, he's an accomplished dealmaker in the business of espionage. He knows something about every spy in the world, or at least he did a few years ago. And secondly, he's married to a high-level government official in the Kremlin who's also a retired member of the Congress of People's Deputies."

"Sounds like you've done your homework, Tony," the president noted. "I hope to God you're right."

The president went around the table, questioning each department head. All agreed that it was worth a try. "Okay then, let's move on it.

"And remember, this thing is close-hold. I don't want any leaks to the press, or this initiative could go right down the toilet and have us facing a diplomatic blunder of huge proportions. And let's not forget why we're doing this. We've got a couple of brave young airmen rotting in a Kremlin prison, and I want 'em back. This group will reconvene in forty-eight hours. Now, let's go to work."

....

Troy was having a sleepless night. He crawled out of his cot and paced around the cold, dank cell, pondering his destiny. He knew that very soon the Soviets would have to either return him to freedom or put him on trial. He sensed that they would prefer the latter because of its propaganda value. He remembered reading how the Soviets rounded up Germans and East Europeans following World War II, sending them to gulags, never to be seen again. He had also read intelligence reports of B-29 crew members shot down during the Korean War and suspected by the

CIA of being held by the Soviet Union. Of course, the Soviets denied the charge.

Damn, he had to stop thinking about these miserable dilemmas. He wished they'd move in another prisoner—anyone. He just wanted someone to talk with.

His next interrogation was set for early in the morning. He had to be sharp to argue with his antagonists. Exhausted, he lay back down on his cot and fell into a restless sleep.

He could see his father playing eight-ball with his cronies at the Smoke House Bar in Bisbee. Then all of a sudden, his father disappeared. But Troy could hear him calling, "Troy, Troy." Troy called back but got no response. The picture cleared, and he saw his father in a strange-looking bed, covered with white sheets and wrapped in some kind of tubing or wires. Troy didn't understand—it didn't make sense.

He cried out, "Are you sick, Papa?" At first there was no reply. Then his father reappeared and began to speak, telling Troy about his heart attack and assuring him that he was okay. His father asked about his captivity, and Troy related what had transpired. It was a joyous and calming exchange between father and son.

Suddenly, Troy's head and shoulder hit the cold concrete floor. He screamed as a sharp pain shot through his injured shoulder. Damn, he hoped he hadn't reinjured it. How could he have been so clumsy? Then he remembered his dream. It had seemed so real. He crawled back onto his cot and manipulated the shoulder like Doctor Khrushova had taught him. As he tried to recall as much of the dream as he could, the pain gradually subsided.

Soon, with a Soviet guard on either side, Troy was marched down the dingy corridor to the interrogation room. He received a surprisingly warm welcome from the chief interrogator, an obese KGB agent with a large neck, and two Soviet Air Force colonels, all who were proficient in English. They seemed relaxed and hospitable, but Troy was suspicious. He knew that they could change personalities in a split second.

The KGB agent started with the same monotonous line of questioning. "Captain Bench, why did you violate Soviet airspace? You are an aggressor, Captain Bench. We Soviets are defenders of freedom."

For weeks, Troy had listened to the same litany of accusations and repetitive questions; he was anxious for a change of pace. Sensing his accusers' relaxed demeanor, he decided to go on the offense. He blurted out, "That's pure propaganda, and you know it."

The metal chair legs scraped the rough concrete floor as the interrogators jerked to attention, eyes widened and brows wrinkled. Troy guessed that they were too startled to speak, so he quickly continued.

"Your socialist republics have imprisoned millions of citizens and charged them with nothing more than disagreeing with your government policies."

As he spoke, he tried to read the faces of his accusers. It was obvious that his verbal attack had thrown them off balance. But what would be their next move? Their eyes bore through him like hot pokers, but the KGB interrogator didn't stop him.

"You've built a wall around your socialist republics to keep your citizens from pursuing freedom. In America we have freedom of speech, and we have freedom to travel when and wherever we want. You don't." Troy sensed that they might actually be listening. "Your regimented Marxist government has stymied creativity, squandered natural resources, and stagnated your economy. Gentlemen, the West will win the Cold War because *we are free.*"

The three officials, led by the KGB agent, jumped to their feet. Red-faced and angry, their fists clenched, the agent shouted to the guards to return Troy to his cell.

Lying on his cot and staring at the ever-burning ceiling light, Troy tried to make sense of the one-sided verbal harangue. If he had made the same comments weeks earlier, he would be lying on his cell floor in a pool of blood or strapped to a gurney heading for the infirmary. What had changed? The interrogator's restrained behavior was unprecedented. Troy anticipated repercussions, but for the moment he reveled in his modest victory. He was proud he had stood up to them.

Suddenly, the corridor door clanged open. He could hear footsteps headed toward his cell.

....

The president convened his Cabinet to discuss the prisoner swap. Glancing at his secretary of state, he asked, "George, what have you and the CIA worked out?"

"Sir, we ran into a brick wall using diplomatic channels, so we switched to a clandestine mode. We persuaded one of the Soviets' top spies, who just happens to be attached to the Soviet delegation at the United Nations, to carry our message. His name is Dmitry Kovtusky."

"My God, you mean we have spies in the sanctimonious halls of the United Nations? What's next?" the president said, laughing. "Well, did this Dmitry fellow get our message to the premier?"

"He did, sir, and the Soviets have agreed, so long as we don't trumpet the swap as a victory. They want the entire exchange downplayed and carried out in a low-key manner."

"That's fine with me, but I'm surprised. The Soviets reveled in the extensive media exposure when our guys were shot down."

"Sir, it seems Orlovsky has become a huge embarrassment to the proud fraternity of Soviet espionage. They *do* want him returned, but I'm not sure he'll be welcomed back to the motherland with loving arms."

"The Soviets surely know that the world press will uncover the details within hours. And if I'm asked, I'm going to tell it like it is."

"Yes sir, that's what I told 'em, so we finally settled for no press releases prior to the exchange. We just need to keep it under wraps until our guys are released."

"George, you know that'll work only as long as there are no leaks. It's going to be tough," the president said. "So what's the plan for the exchange?"

"Sir, it'll take place at eight o'clock Sunday morning at Checkpoint Charlie in Berlin. Captain Bench and Lieutenant Olson will arrive in civilian suits, as will Orlovsky. A Soviet Army colonel and an American Air Force colonel will handle the exchange and sign for their respective prisoners."

The president went around the table querying each department secretary for potential problems. The attorney general said that he'd arrange for Orlovsky to be brought from the federal penitentiary in New York to Andrews AFB, where the Air Force would fly him on to Tempelhof in Berlin.

The secretary of defense said that he'd make arrangements for Captain Bench and Lieutenant Olson to be flown to Andrews after the exchange. At Andrews they would be given medical evaluations and debriefed by military intelligence and the CIA. They would also be instructed by public affairs officials in preparation for a press conference to take place on about the fifth day.

"How about the wives?" the president asked.

"I'll arrange to have them flown to Washington," the secretary of defense said.

"George, I want State to handle all press relations. And based on the Soviet sensitivity in this matter, let's keep it under our hats until we have Bench and Olson in tow."

The president pressed the intercom button on his desk. "Dorothy, set up a conference call with Mrs. Bench and Mrs. Olson."

"Yes, Mr. President."

Troy's cell door screeched as it slid open. The two Soviet Air Force colonels who had interrogated him earlier entered his tiny cell, along with two heavy-set, uniformed guards. "You need to lubricate that damn door—it's keeping me awake," Troy said with a smile, still in high spirits from his recent encounter. The somber group ignored his attempt at humor.

"You will come with us now, Captain," one of the colonels ordered.

They took a circuitous route through a maze of dark, narrow catacombs with damp, rough-hewn walls that reminded Troy of the copper-mine tunnels beneath Bisbee. Based on the glum mood of his escorts, he guessed that he might be on his way to a military trial.

After a lengthy walk, they passed through a nondescript metal door into a small, carpeted room with a dark hardwood table and half a dozen upholstered chairs. Colorful paintings of Soviet tanks in combat posture adorned the walls.

The colonels motioned Troy to be seated. After several minutes of tense silence, the door opened and both colonels jumped to rigid attention. Troy stood. An older military officer with a shock of thick, white hair; a reddish, pockmarked face; and a colorful array of combat medals dangling from his Army uniform sat down at the head of the table.

In broken but understandable English, the officer introduced himself as Colonel General Vladimir Bugovia, commander of the Moscow Military District. Facing Troy in his swivel chair, he said, "I have surprise for you, Captain Bench."

Turning toward the door, he shouted something in Russian. The door swung open, and broad smiles enveloped two American fliers' faces. Troy Bench and Carl Olson had at last been reunited. "Damn, you look great, Carl," Troy said as they hugged and wiped away tears.

General Bugovia gestured for the Americans to

sit. "I have news for you. To show the compassion and generosity of the peoples of the Union of Soviet Socialist Republics, we have pardoned you for your aggressive act of intrusion into Soviet airspace and relieved you of your crimes against the motherland. All criminal charges are forgiven. On Sunday morning you will be turned over to the American military in Berlin."

Troy was stunned, and he could see Carl felt the same. Immediately he expected that there must be conditions attached. "General, we will sign *no* papers or confessions of any kind."

"Captain Bench, confession is not necessary. The motherland forgives you both for your crimes."

That evening Troy and Carl were ushered into upgraded overnight quarters with real beds and a bathtub. Laid out on the beds were what appeared to be two ill-fitting, dark blue suits with equally drab ties and white shirts. Troy laughed. "These things look like something out of an old Marx Brothers movie, but they sure as hell beat the baggy, striped pajamas we've been living in."

"Maybe we can start a new fashion trend," Carl said, laughing.

That night they were served a tough but tasty pan-fried roast with vegetables, along with a bottle of Russian vodka. They each had one drink and talked for hours. Aware that their room was more than likely bugged, they were careful not to discuss anything military. Instead they talked about their wives, Carl's little girls, and several memorable games they had played when they were both on the Air Force Academy football team.

They spent a restless night—exhausted, but too excited to sleep and wary that something could still go awry.

The following morning they were served a breakfast of fried eggs and ham. While they were squeezing into their Marx Brothers suits, a guard opened the door and Doctor Helga Khrushova entered.

"I am on my way to the infirmary, but I have small gift for your wives—something I made." She handed each officer a small package wrapped in brown paper and tied with white twine. "I hope in later years that these hand-stitched doilies will remind you and your families of a time past in U.S.–Soviet relations." Both officers clasped Doctor Khrushova's hands warmly and thanked her for healing their wounds. She seemed surprised, but appeared to welcome the gesture.

"Doctor, I hope you will visit America someday. And when you do, Carl and I will have a huge welcome mat out for you. Thank you so much for everything."

Colonel General Bugovia drove with them to a deserted part of the Vnukovo military airdrome in northwest Moscow, where they boarded a small twin-engine turboprop transport for the four-hour flight to East Berlin. Accompanied by the general and four husky armed guards, Troy surmised that the general had been given responsibility for ensuring their safe passage to Berlin.

The flight was uncomfortably cold and noisy. The aircraft had no insulation or padding between the riveted aluminum sheathing and the passenger compartment. Old newspapers were taped over the porthole windows to eliminate any chance for a view of the Soviet landscape or military installations.

Troy noticed that the general also seemed irritated with the condition of the airplane. A one-sided discussion ensued between him and the chief pilot, with a lot of arm-waving by the general and a lot of standing at rigid attention by the chief pilot. *A cogent demonstration of Soviet military discipline*, Troy thought. Troy was concerned that something might still go wrong.

Upon landing at an isolated airstrip in the Soviet sector of the four-power controlled city, Troy and Carl were driven with the general and two guards in a black Mercedes limousine. Troy was taken aback by the roads void of cars and people and the run-down, drab appearance of the city's streets and buildings. They were dropped off at an embassy-style hotel in the center of East Berlin and hustled to a third-floor room with two beds and a common bathroom at the end of a short hall. Two guards were stationed outside their door.

That night they dined in the hotel dining room with General Bugovia and a high-ranking, at-large Soviet diplomat. Both men tried to draw Troy and Carl into a discussion of communism vs. democracy, but the Americans had decided earlier not to get into any sensitive dialogue that might upset their hosts. Instead, they easily coaxed the general into talking about his World War II combat exploits commanding a tank battalion in defense of Leningrad.

After a hearty breakfast on Sunday morning, they were driven in the Mercedes down Friedrichstrasse to a point one hundred meters from an insignificant-looking white, wooden shack. The general told them to walk slowly down the street toward the guard shack. After shaking the general's hand, and then stepping back and saluting him, Troy and Carl followed his instructions.

Starting toward Checkpoint Charlie, they spotted an American Air Force colonel walking toward them with a broad smile.

Troy turned to Carl with a huge smile of his own. "I think we can relax now. I believe our nightmare is over."

Chapter XXII

AIR FORCE COLONEL BRADLEY Meyers scribbled a brusque signature on a Soviet transfer document, and Sergei Orlovsky was ushered past Checkpoint Charlie into the Soviet sector. Troy and Carl entered the Western Zone and were whisked off by staff car to Tempelhof Airport, where they boarded a waiting, silver-and-blue Boeing 707 from the Special Air Mission fleet at Andrews AFB, Maryland. The airplane, with a large American flag painted on its tail and the words "United States of America" emboldened across its upper fuselage, was an uplifting reminder for Troy that he was almost home. Because it was normally used in conjunction with presidential travel to transport the press corps and support personnel, the plane was outfitted with conversational areas, tables and comfortable seating.

Colonel Jack Sparks, on-location commander of the Shark Bite operation at SAC headquarters and Eielson AFB, and Lieutenant Colonel Stan Zuko from SAC intelligence heartily welcomed the officers as they boarded. Troy and Carl quickly settled in and buckled their seatbelts, as the 707 crew wasted no time in getting airborne.

An Air Force steward asked what they would like to drink. Troy and Carl each ordered a beer.

"General Strong asked me to accompany you on your return flight to the States and update you on what's happened in the world during the last two months," Colonel Sparks said.

He led off with the question uppermost on Troy's mind: What was the reaction by the Pentagon and by the American people to the shoot-down, and how much consternation and diplomatic upheaval had the incident caused? Colonel Sparks assured the officers that the Air Force and the president were completely accepting of the mission and that the American people simply demanded their swift return. "Rest assured, you and your crew did exactly what you were asked to do, and you performed that mission with skill and courage."

"But, Colonel, I lost one of my best friends—a fine Air Force officer and pilot."

"Believe me, Captain, I understand your anguish at the loss of a best friend. But the business we're in is a dangerous one. I want both of you officers to remember this: the intelligence gleaned from your

mission will save countless lives if we ever—God for-
bid—have to go to war with the Soviet Union. Lieutenant Bill Candee's death was not in vain."

Lieutenant Colonel Zuko looked fervently at both
fliers. "Your penetration mission provided us with
such significant electronic intelligence that we took
immediate steps to integrate the data into the SAC
war plans."

Staring at his empty beer can and speaking deliberately, Troy asked, "Sir, what's going to happen to us
when we land?"

"We'll talk about that after you take a shower and
get out of those funny-looking Commie suits. Your
wives provided us with fresh Air Force uniforms.
They're laid out for you on your beds."

"Beds? Showers? We're in an airplane, Colonel!"
Carl blurted out.

"Lieutenant, the president said nothing's too good
for you two, so he lent us one of his specially outfitted
support airplanes. Get cleaned up and then we'll talk
more. By the way, go easy on the water—the supply
is limited."

After a shave and shower, Troy donned his loose-
fitting uniform and felt like he was back in the Air
Force—it was a warm, comfortable feeling. For the
next couple of hours, the colonels updated Troy and
Carl. They were surprised to learn that their intern-
ment had been the subject of almost daily national

press coverage—most of it positive, but some negative as well.

Colonel Sparks briefed them on their schedule for the week. "Your wives arrived last evening and are waiting for you in the VIP quarters at Andrews," he said with a smile. "Tomorrow's a free day for you—nothing's planned. Tuesday morning you'll get a quick physical, and then in the afternoon you'll meet with the Pentagon intelligence folks, which could stretch into Wednesday. Thursday morning you and your wives are scheduled for thirty minutes with the president."

"Did you say ... the president?" Troy asked, momentarily confused.

"That's right, you're meeting with the president of the United States and the first lady."

As Troy tried to digest this information, Colonel Sparks continued. "Thursday afternoon you'll have a half-hour press conference at the Pentagon. The Pentagon's public relations people will prep you prior to the meeting. Friday will be a free day, and then Saturday you'll be flown back to your respective bases to start a thirty-day convalescent leave. Is there anything you would like to see or do while you're in Washington?"

"Yes, sir, there is," Troy said. "Carl and I need to visit a friend at Arlington."

"That can be arranged," the colonel said with a

nod. So that's it, gentlemen. You pretty much belong to us for the next week."

As the crew prepared for landing, Troy asked the aircraft commander if he and Carl could sit in the crew compartment for the landing. The pilot was happy to oblige.

After they touched down and were taxiing to the parking ramp, Troy noticed a crowd gathered in front of base ops.

He commented to the pilot, "Some VIP must be arriving."

"Yeah, you're right, Captain," the pilot said with a chuckle, "and I believe you two are the VIPs they're expecting."

Chills raced up and down Troy's spine. Neither he nor Carl were ready to meet the public; they only wanted to see their families.

Colonel Sparks sensed their uneasiness. "Don't worry, I'll handle it. All you need to say is something like 'We're happy to be home, and we want to thank everyone for their support. Right now we just want to be with our families.' I'll take care of the rest. An Air Force driver and staff car are standing by in front of base ops to take you to your quarters."

Before they deplaned, Troy and Carl thanked each member of the flight crew for their help and courtesy.

....

By military standards, the VIP quarters at Andrews

were luxurious: cherry wood paneling and cabinets throughout, with wall-to-wall plush carpeting. Troy and Carl thought they were in paradise—especially with no light bulb in the ceiling to keep them awake all night.

Although knowing that Wendy was approaching her eighth month, Troy was still surprised at just how pregnant she appeared. He embraced her carefully as if she were a porcelain doll. "Troy, darling, I'm fine, stop treating me like an invalid. I'm just having a baby. The doctor even said we could make love if we're careful."

"You mean we can have some wild and crazy sex?" Troy teased.

"Not quite. We need to postpone the wild and crazy part until after the baby's born."

They turned the lights low and gently made love—then held each other and talked for hours. It was well past midnight when they fell asleep in each other's arms. Troy awoke several times during the night, not yet comfortable in a darkened room. Cradling Wendy in his arms, he realized how lucky he was to be alive: there were so many times he had very nearly given in to his interrogators ... the physical pain of his interrogations had been almost more than he could bear ... and he came close to believing his captors when they told him over and over again that he would never be released and was on his way to a gulag. He thanked God for bringing him home.

The phone awakened Troy and Wendy a little after ten o'clock the next morning.

"Hey, it's Linda. Can you guys join us for an early lunch? Let's meet at the club at 11 o'clock, okay?

Before leaving for the club, Troy called his parents. His father had recuperated enough to return to Bisbee following heart surgery at the Tucson Medical Center.

His father answered the phone, and then shouted, "Mama, it's Troy! Troy, it's so good to hear your voice. Hey, Troy, guess what? Mama and I watched you on the television last night. You didn't say much, but I'm sure you had lots on your mind." His father stopped to take a breath, then continued. "Troy, I have to tell you … something strange happened to me during my operation."

"I know, Papa. Wendy told me. I also have something that I need to share with you that happened to me about the same time. But Papa, I have a thirty-day convalescent leave starting in a week. Wendy and I plan on spending a few days in Bisbee with the family." Troy told his father to continue getting well and ended the call with a meaningful "I love you."

The week moved quickly, with Troy and Carl keeping busy from morning until evening. During the day, Wendy and Linda took guided tours around

Washington and shopped for dresses to wear for the visit with the president. The four of them got together each evening for dinner, and their friendship grew.

Troy was surprised when the Pentagon intelligence agencies verified what Colonel Sparks had said on the plane: the data collected from their flight over the Soviet peninsula, particularly the last ten minutes of the mission, was so valuable that nuclear war plans had been revised to reflect the new information.

The Pentagon public affairs officials did a good job preparing Troy and Carl for questions from the press corps and advising them on what classified data they could not discuss. The men's humility, straightforwardness, and timely humor impressed the journalists. At the end of the session, the press corps stood and applauded.

The scariest part of the week was the anticipation of meeting with the president and his wife. Alas, that fear proved groundless. The president and his wife were so gracious and easygoing that the two couples relaxed immediately.

Troy thanked the president for his help in obtaining their release and apologized for causing all the trouble.

"You have that wrong, Captain Bench," the president said firmly. "It is you two we must thank. You could have turned away from the threat area much sooner, but our war planners wouldn't have had the valuable intelligence data you exposed." Troy was impressed with how quickly the president put everyone in the room at ease. "I'm terribly sorry Lieutenant Candee can't be here with us today. I know how much you must miss him. This nation owes the three of you a huge debt of gratitude, and we honor your skill and bravery."

The president paused to clear his throat. "There's something else I want to say. We often forget how important the wives are to professional soldiers, sailors, or airmen. I want to thank you, Wendy and Linda, for your determination and strength throughout this ordeal. I can't award you a medal, but I do have something I would like to present to you ladies from my wife and me."

The president handed two silver trays to Wendy and Linda, each with the deep blue-and-tan presidential seal embedded in the center, and the inscription:

Thank you for your strength and your service.
—The President of the United States.

....

Friday morning, a staff car drove Troy and Carl across the Potomac and on to the hallowed grounds of Arlington National Cemetery. Troy gazed out the windows at row upon row of white marble headstones. "This humbles the strongest of us. These people gave their lives for us. It's such a sacred place and so inspiring," Troy said somberly. "It's a place where valor rests."

"And there's about a quarter-million brave souls, from the lowliest buck-private to presidents and five-star generals, entombed here," Carl added. "Bill is surely in good company."

Locating Lieutenant Candee's burial site, they knelt beside the grave and for a time said nothing—praying, each in his own way. Then they thought up funny quips and sayings Bill Candee had spoken that had kept them in stitches. They laughed and knew Bill Candee was laughing with them.

Later they stood at attention and executed a slow, solemn salute—then turned and walked away. Neither Troy nor Carl spoke for a time. No words were adequate.

Chapter XXIII

SATURDAY MORNING TROY, CARL, and their wives took a staff car to Washington National Airport for a commercial flight to their respective bases. It was a happy time—they were going home; the ordeal was over. It was also an emotional time; they had become best friends while living through the trauma of the last two months. They realized the harsh adventure that had drawn them together would keep them close for the rest of their lives.

....

Mark Denman, Troy's old friend, met Troy and Wendy at the Los Angeles International Airport. While picking up their baggage, Troy was confronted by inquisitive reporters from the *Los Angeles Times* and *San Francisco Chronicle*: "Captain Bench, were you on a spy mission? Were you in international airspace or over Soviet territory when you were shot down?" they demanded.

"I addressed those questions at a press conference in Washington two days ago," Troy said firmly. "You'll have to contact the Pentagon public affairs people for any further information. Please ... if you don't mind, my wife and I would like to go home now."

After Troy finally allowed a few photos, the reporters apologized for the intrusion and wished the couple a happy homecoming.

With Wendy asleep in the backseat, Mark drove and updated Troy on what had been going on in the bomb wing during the last few months. He said the scuttlebutt was that the B-47s at March would soon be retired to the boneyard at Davis-Monthan and the wing would convert to B-52s within a year. Some pilots and bomb-navs would transfer to other B-47 bases, but the majority would remain at March and transition into the new, eight-engine B-52 bomber.

"What do *you* want to do, Mark?" Troy asked.

"I haven't decided. It depends in which airplane I can get the fastest upgrade to aircraft commander. I want to get a crew, Troy; I'm getting tired of flying copilot."

"I can certainly understand that," Troy said. "Was there any talk about SAC releasing pilots to go to fighter outfits?"

Mark chuckled. "Yeah, one brave son of a bitch

stood up at a recent briefing by SAC headquarters and asked that question. You'd've thought the guy had asked to get into heaven. He was told by the briefing colonel never to bring that up again: 'This is SAC, son, and this is where you're staying.'"

Mark dropped Troy and Wendy off at their Riverside apartment, which the Officers' Wives Club had stocked with enough food to last for at least a week. The couple thanked Mark for the ride.

"You're welcome," Mark said. "And if I were you guys, I'd unplug the phone and leave the lights off for the next couple of days."

Wendy had done a good job screening the mail, discarding the superfluous stuff and retaining only what she thought would interest Troy. There was also a small pile of mail that arrived while she was away. Most of it was from well-wishers welcoming Troy back and thanking him for service to his country. A few could be categorized as "hate mail," chastising him for spying on the peaceful Soviets. Those went in the trash.

Then Troy's eyes zeroed in on one envelope with an IBM logo. Ripping it open, he saw that it was from Stewart Brown. It read, in part:

Dear Troy,
I can't tell you how pleased Betty and I were to hear of your release and return to the States. ... The IBM job offer still stands. ... Betty and I would like to meet

you and Wendy for lunch in Riverside or Los Angeles at
your convenience.
Sincerely,
Stewart

Troy thought, *Now, there's something else to consider.*

A phone call from his squadron commander, Lieutenant Colonel Jack Blauw, interrupted his thoughts. "Troy, it's good to have you back. Could you stop by the squadron Tuesday morning to go over a couple of personnel matters? It won't take long."

"Yes, sir, I'll be there."

Wendy and Troy spent the rest of the day putting the house back into order. On Sunday they drove to Wendy's parents' farm in Anaheim. The next morning they indulged in one of their favorite pastimes: sampling her parents' wines and walking through the vineyards.

Troy found it difficult to sit still and concentrate. His mind kept darting back to the shoot-down and Bill Candee. *Did Bill have a quick death? Had he struggled? Just how did he die?* Troy guessed that he'd probably never know the answers.

At nine o'clock Tuesday morning, Troy drove into the parking lot outside the 64th Bomb Squadron building at March. Everything seemed strange and surreal: the location of the trash cans, the paint on the exterior walls, even the shadows on the buildings appeared to have changed. It seemed like years, rather than months, since he'd been in the building. He was anxious about how he'd be accepted back into the squadron. Would people blame him for Bill's death?

As he walked down the long entry hall, his concerns were laid to rest. He was greeted warmly and enthusiastically welcomed. Several crew members mentioned they were sorry to hear about Bill, but they didn't seem to hold Troy at fault.

Troy knocked on the squadron commander's door. "Come in," Colonel Blauw called out. "Oh, it's you, Troy. Please come in and take a seat."

Blauw pulled a chair alongside his desk and thrust his hand forward to welcome Troy. "It's really good to see you. You look great. How ya feeling?"

"I'm fine, sir. I'm still a little tired, and my uniform's a little baggy, but I'll gain weight again and get back in shape soon."

"Troy, I don't want to waste your time—I know you have a lot to do, so I'll get to the point. The wing got a call from General Strong's executive officer last Friday. General Strong is sending a KC-135 down for you and Wendy to fly to SAC headquarters at Omaha on Thursday morning. Lieutenant Olson and his family and Bill Candee's parents will be there. Think the general wants to hang some medals on you all."

"Sir, I don't want to seem ungrateful, but couldn't we just do it here in the privacy of your office?"

"I'm afraid not, Troy. I believe this is a command performance by SAC headquarters.

"Another thing before I forget it: have you given any thought to what you want to do next? I mean, do you want to stay in bombers and go to B-52s, or would you like to go to grad school and get a master's in engineering? This could be a chance to write your own ticket; few officers have that opportunity. I think you need to ponder those questions. General Strong might just want to know."

"Thank you, sir, I will. And thanks for the heads-up."

When told about the trip to Omaha later that afternoon, Wendy was less than enthusiastic. She was in her thirty-fourth week but knew they couldn't easily refuse a four-star general's invitation.

Wendy and Linda touched base over the phone and decided that they'd spent enough money on their "presidential dresses" to justify wearing them again. After all, nobody in Omaha had seen them and Wendy wasn't about to splurge for another expensive maternity outfit.

Thursday morning a KC-135 flew Troy and Wendy to Offutt AFB in a little less than three hours. Wendy experienced some discomfort during the flight, but by the time they landed she felt better. Troy and Wendy were happy to meet Carl and Linda and their little girls, Megan and Sara, in the lobby. Though they'd been apart for only a few days, it felt good to be to-gether again. Also in the lobby were Mr. and Mrs. William Candee.

Mr. Candee was a tall, rawboned rancher, well over six foot and somewhere in his early fifties. His gray snakeskin boots displayed his hand-tooled cattle brand. A western shirt with white pearl snaps down the front, a tailored brown suede coat, and a cream-colored Stetson rounded out his North Texas attire. Like his son, the senior Candee had a ready smile and a wit to match. Bill Candee's mother was a statuesque, well-groomed woman with a diamond wedding ring the size of an ice cube.

"I'm Bill Candee, and this is my wife, Charlene. Sure glad to finally make y'all's acquaintance."

"You have to be Troy," Mrs. Candee smiled as she wrapped her arms around Troy. "Bill Junior always spoke so highly of you, Troy. And this beautiful soon-to-be mom has to be Wendy." She gave Wendy a hug and then turned to the rest of the group. "And you must be Carl and Linda Olson. Oh, and your darling little girls, Megan and Sara." Mrs. Candee bent down and hugged each of them.

"If y'all don't mind, let's go sit in the lounge for a spell and get acquainted," Mr. Candee suggested.

"If you wonderful people will excuse me," Wendy said, "I believe this big lump in my belly and I need a little rest." She turned away and motioned Troy that she would be in the room.

"Do you want me to go with you, honey?" Troy asked.

"No, I'll be fine. I just need to rest this body for a bit." She blew him a kiss as she headed for their quarters.

Soon after being served drinks in the lounge, Mr. Candee offered a toast.

"I know Bill Junior is watching and wishing he were here." Raising his glass of Jack Daniels on ice and squeezing Charlene's hand, Mr. Candee said, "Here's to you, Billy, from your family and your good friends."

With that he tipped his head back and downed the glass of straight whiskey.

Mr. Candee continued, "I have something I need to say to y'all. Charlene and I have always been proud of our Bill Junior. We were proud of him when he captained the Texas Tech football team. We were proud when he became an Air Force officer and pilot. And we were proud of him as a rancher. He loved the ranch. He sat his quarterhorse, Roscoe, like a glove...." Mr. Candee's voice drifted off as his eyes filled with tears.

After a moment, he gathered his composure and spoke firmly and clearly. "We hold no one, except the Soviets, responsible for Billy's death. Troy, Billy once told his mother and me that flying with you was one of the best things that ever happened to him, even though you were an Academy puke—I believe that's the way he put it—and not a Texas Tech Red Raider."

He paused and gave a self-deprecating laugh. "Charlene and I want you to know that we're certain you did everything possible that day to save your crew."

Tears welled up in Troy's eyes. "Thank you, sir. Bill was a fine pilot and a very close friend, and I'll never forget him."

They all raised their glasses in a salute to Bill.

....

Friday morning everyone gathered in General Strong's mahogany-paneled office at SAC headquarters. A lieutenant briefed them on where to stand and what the protocol for the presentation ceremony would be.

General Strong entered the room and greeted each person warmly. When he got to Troy, he said, "This is becoming a habit, Captain Bench."

The general presented each officer with a Distinguished Flying Cross (Troy's second) and a Purple Heart. Mr. and Mrs. Candee received Lieutenant Candee's awards posthumously. The general also presented Troy with a Bronze Star with a *V* device for valor. Due to the high classification of the mission, the citations read generically. The true text was placed in a classified folder to be made public at some future time.

After a thirty-minute social reception in an adjoining room, the general invited Troy and Carl back into his office for a private session. Colonel Bill Barnes, director of officer assignments for SAC, joined them.

"Gentlemen, I want you to be candid about the direction you'd like your Air Force careers to go. I want to know what you'd like for an assignment—you've certainly earned special treatment." The general nodded toward Troy.

"General, as you know, I've always wanted to fly fighters," Troy responded. I'd like to go to an F-4 fighter outfit."

"Yes, Captain Bench. I *do* remember telling you once that we'd think about that at a later time."

Colonel Barnes leaned over and whispered something in the general's ear.

"Oh yes, I almost forgot, Captain Olson, you're out of uniform; you've been promoted."

The general reached in his pocket and pulled out a pair of shiny captain bars.

Troy leaned over, smiled, and shook Carl's hand.

"So, Captain Olson, what would you like for an assignment?"

"General, thank you, sir," Carl stammered. "Wow, it's ... ah ... so unexpected. I seem to have lost my train of thought." Carl shook his head as if to clear it. "Sir, my degree's in aerospace engineering. My choice would be to pursue a master's degree in AE through the Air Force Institute of Technology."

The general glanced toward Colonel Barnes. "Bill, go see what you can do for these officers."

"Yes, sir, I'll be right back."

"While we're waiting on Colonel Barnes, I want to talk to you about how the services, and particularly the Air Force, are going to fit into the nation's air and space strategy for which the Air Force now has prime responsibility. All of the services—Army, Navy, and the Air Force—are becoming more 'purple suited.' By that, I mean we're all developing plans to work closer together on land, sea, air, and space operations. The Pentagon's going to be conducting a lot of joint operations where the three services function almost as one. We need Air Force officers cross-trained in how the Army and Navy function and vice versa. We need to learn more about each service's strengths and weaknesses and how we can best assist each other. The next war will demand that.

"And talking about the next war, the Indochina area—and particularly a little country called Vietnam—is heating up. We may be asked to provide assistance against the Communist aggression from the North if the president so determines.

"We're going to need bright, young, and dedicated

leaders like you in our future Air Force—leaders who can work with other services and function as comfortably in space as we now do in our own atmosphere."

Colonel Barnes returned with a folder in his hand. "Okay, Bill, what've you got?" General Strong asked.

"Sir, Captain Olson will attend Purdue University in the fall semester to pursue a masters in aerospace engineering."

The general reached out and shook Carl's hand. "Congratulations, Captain. And how about Captain Bench?"

"Captain Bench will attend the Fighter Upgrade Training School at Nellis Air Force Base, with a follow-on assignment to an F-4 fighter wing. However, before that, he'll attend the Armed Forces Staff College in Virginia for six months, where he'll study joint defense operations with equal numbers of Army, Navy and Marine officers."

"Well, gentlemen, you got what you asked for," General Strong said. "It won't happen again—make the most of it."

Troy and Carl were all smiles. They thanked General Strong for the dream assignments, and assured him they would definitely make the most of them.

Chapter XXIV

Everyone said their good-byes and returned to their quarters to pack up and leave Omaha. The occasion had been heartwarming but also emotional. Mr. and Mrs. Candee invited both families to visit their North Texas ranch. "I promise that Megan and Sara will be riding a horse all by themselves after two days," Mr. Candee said. "I guarantee it."

With the girls jumping up and down in excitement, Carl agreed to visit the ranch within the next six months.

....

A KC-135 tanker was scheduled to fly Troy and Wendy back to March AFB following the ceremony. Wendy had felt a few random contractions from the busy activities of the day and asked Troy to check on the availability of a medevac going their direction.

After hanging up the phone, Troy sat down next

to her and held her hand. "Honey, there's a medevac leaving in the morning with three stops before March. With you having contractions, I think we should play it safe and take the medevac. If anything happens, we'll have qualified medical personnel onboard."

Wendy squeezed Troy's hand to reassure him, as well as herself, that she'd be okay. She didn't want to wait another day and risk having the baby so far from home. "I'll be fine, Troy. They're just those Braxton Hicks practice contractions." At least she hoped they were. "Let's stick with the tanker and get home today."

Severe weather in the Omaha area delayed takeoff for another three hours. The KC-135 finally got airborne five hours after Troy and Wendy had arrived at base ops. The flight was planned as a training mission for the tanker, which was scheduled to refuel a B-52 a half hour after takeoff.

The Air Force and Boeing designed the KC-135 to offload fuel, not to carry passengers; inside, it was primitive, noisy, and uncomfortable.

Finally airborne, and with help from the crew chief, Troy rigged a makeshift bed of sorts and helped Wendy lie on her side as her doctor had recommended. After assuring Troy she would be fine, he went forward to the cockpit. He thought he recognized the aircraft commander's name, Paul McMurkle, as a fellow student in pilot training. They had not seen each other for several years.

As they reminisced, the crew chief rushed into the cockpit. "Captain Bench, excuse me, sir, but I think you'd better come quick—your wife's having trouble breathing."

Troy raced to Wendy's side and felt an icy fear wash over his body. Wendy was breathing fast and grimacing in pain.

"Honey, what is it?" he pleaded.

"The contractions … they're really strong and coming closer together."

"Chief, I need an oxygen hose extension and a mask for my wife right away," Troy shouted over the din of the airplane noise.

Placing the oxygen mask on her face, Troy had the crew chief set the regulator to 100 percent. "Chief, tell Lieutenant McMurkle that I believe my wife's going to have a baby any time now. We need to get on the ground and get her to a hospital—fast!"

The tanker was in the middle of offloading twenty thousand pounds of JP-4 to a B-52, and the residual fumes in the cabin weren't helping Wendy's nausea.

"Napa Three-zero, we have an emergency on-board. We need to terminate refueling and get on the ground ASAP," McMurkle advised the B-52 pilot.

"Roger, Bingo Two-one, understand. We've got

enough gas for our mission, so we'll be on our way. Good luck with your emergency."

The crew chief, back from the cockpit, told Troy that Lieutenant McMurkle wanted to talk with him over the interphone.

"Troy, how's your wife doing?" McMurkle asked.

"Not well. She's having trouble breathing, and I don't think the baby's going to wait. Her contractions are becoming more frequent. I'm really worried, Paul," Troy said in frustration. "I don't know a damn thing about delivering a baby."

"Troy, I'm diverting to Lowry Air Force Base, in the center of Denver. The University of Colorado Medical Center is only about ten minutes from the base. I've declared an emergency and advised the base to have a doctor and an ambulance meet us when we turn off the runway. And, Troy, I've got this baby pegged at 480 knots. Lowry has cleared traffic, and we've been given a straight-in approach. We should be on the ground in less than thirty minutes."

Troy could hear people speaking in the background as McMurkle paused. "Hang on a second, Troy. I may have some help for you."

"Okay ... yes, okay ... Troy, Staff Sergeant Henderson, my boom operator, just told me he was a paramedic in Dallas for a short time before joining the Air Force. He's on his way back to do what he can."

"Thanks, Paul."

"I'm Staff Sergeant Henderson, sir."

Troy quickly shook his hand. "What's your first name, Sergeant?"

"Dave, sir."

"Okay, Dave, it's you and me. We're gonna do this together. My wife, Wendy, is at thirty-five weeks. She hasn't had any out-of-the-ordinary medical problems to speak of, and she's otherwise healthy. I'm taking orders from *you*, now, Dave. You tell me what to do."

Just then Wendy grabbed Troy's arm in a death grip. "Troy, help me, the baby's coming!" She screamed, panting through another contraction. "Oh, no! Troy, my water just broke!"

Troy felt like his heart was going to burst through his chest. "Honey, this is Sergeant Dave Henderson," he said, trying to sound calm. "He was a paramedic before joining the Air Force. He's going to help you."

Wendy, now covered in sweat, jerked the oxygen mask off her face. "I'm so uncomfortable," she said, grimacing.

"Wendy, I want you to focus on your breathing," Dave said in a soothing voice. "The baby needs the extra oxygen at this altitude. Breathe with me, in ... two, three, four, and out ... two, three, four. You're doing fine, Wendy," Dave reassured her.

"Captain, I'm gonna need some supplies," Dave said, looking up at Troy. "All the clean sheets, towels, and blankets you can find. I also need a med pack with some sterile gloves right away. Then I need you to head to the galley and boil a knife and a pair of shoelaces in water for three minutes. If you can find an extra one, cut a one-foot section of oxygen tubing and boil it, too. I'll use that to suction the baby if necessary. And sir, please hurry."

Troy raced off to gather the items, chastising himself as he went for not insisting they wait and take the medevac. If anything happened to Wendy or the baby, he could never forgive himself. He heard Dave shouting to the crew chief to rig a privacy curtain from some folded canvas stacked nearby. Troy returned and quickly set down the supplies. "Now, with your permission, ma'am," Dave said, "I'd like to see where this baby is."

Troy and Dave removed the soaked blankets under Wendy and placed a clean blanket over her waist and legs for privacy. Troy helped Wendy pull off her underwear as Dave ripped open an onboard med pack and donned a pair of sterile gloves. As gently as possible, Dave checked whether she was dilated. To his dismay, she had completely dilated. The baby was coming fast, but at least the little one's head was down.

Wendy stifled a scream. "I need to push! There's too much pressure!"

"Honey, hold on, we're only twenty minutes from Lowry," Troy pleaded.

"Troy, I'm not going to meet your timetable. I'm having this baby *now*!"

Troy searched Dave's face for confirmation. "Sorry, sir, the baby's already crowning."

It'd been a long time since Dave had assisted in a birth, and he'd never delivered one on his own, much less under such trying conditions. He was nervous, but he couldn't let Troy or Wendy see his fear. He knew that thirty-five weeks was on the borderline of lung maturity. *This baby may not be able to breathe on its own*, he thought. He prayed that Wendy's calculations were off and that the baby was closer to thirty-seven weeks.

The next contraction engulfed Wendy in pain, but instinct took over and she started pushing.

"Okay, Wendy, good job!" Dave counted slowly to ten to help her control her pushing. "I see a beautiful head," he announced.

With that encouragement, Wendy gave a strong, long push on the next contraction.

"Great job, honey," Troy said. He was amazed to see the large, glistening head of his baby. A feeling of pride crept over his body, but he knew the baby was not yet out of danger.

"On this next push, Wendy, I need you to stop pushing when I tell you. I'm going to suction the baby's mouth," Dave explained. The fluid was clear, so he didn't think he needed to suction the stomach.

After gently suctioning the mouth with the oxygen tubing, Dave was ready to deliver the shoulders and the rest of Baby Bench on the next contraction.

"Ready, Wendy?" Dave felt her belly tightening with the contraction. "Puuuusssshhh! Puuuussssshhh!"

Something was wrong. The shoulders weren't coming out. Adding to the difficulty, the airplane was encountering some severe turbulence.

"Captain, you need to push her knees up toward her chest and out, *now!*" Dave shouted over the din of aircraft noise. "Wendy, you need to help him by pulling back on your knees.

"I need more clearance. This baby is bigger than I thought. Captain, push back harder, *now.*"

Dave knew the baby could die if he couldn't get the shoulders out.

On the next contraction, while Wendy pushed, Dave pressed firmly on her pelvis. To his relief, the first glorious shoulder appeared. *Thank God*, he thought. With gentle traction, Dave put a thumb under the remaining shoulder and the whole baby was suddenly in his hands. He had forgotten how slippery new babies were—he held on for dear life. And finally, they heard a feeble cry, followed by a strong wail that was music to everyone's ears.

"Sir, ma'am, you have a brand-new baby boy. Congratulations!" Dave couldn't help but smile as he laid baby Jack Steven Bench on Wendy's belly. He looked toward Troy and saw him wiping tears from his eyes.

Dave tied off the cord with two boiled shoelaces, and then handed a disinfected knife to Troy and directed him to cut between the tie offs. Troy hadn't realized the umbilical cord was like trying to cut a carburetor hose—it was thick and rubbery. To be on the safe side, Dave took the oxygen mask off Wendy's mouth. He placed the regulator to 100 percent and on pressure, and let it blow across Wendy's and Jack's faces. Watching the new baby boy nuzzle up to Wendy's chest, Dave was sure that little Jack was at least thirty-seven weeks.

Troy turned toward Sergeant Dave Henderson. "Dave, thank you, sir. You'll always be a welcome part of our family."

Her face lined with exhaustion, Wendy reached over, clasped her hand around Dave's arm, and smiled.

....

The big tanker coasted to a smooth landing, turned off the Lowry runway, and stopped. Wendy and baby Jack Bench were taken by stretcher, along with an attending Lowry physician, to a waiting Air Force ambulance. Dave and Troy accompanied the trio to the University of Colorado Medical Center where the baby was pronounced in fine shape. The hospital staff praised Dave for his accurate medical decisions under adverse conditions.

....

The following day, *The Denver Post* headline read, "Cold War hero helps deliver his son onboard SAC tanker followed by emergency landing at Lowry AFB."

Colonel Bill Barnes brought a copy of *The Denver Post* into General Strong's office. The general looked at it in amazement. "For God's sake, will that boy ever stop making headlines?"

When advised of the news, the president said, "Wonderful," and buzzed his secretary. "Dorothy, get a gift for my wife and me to send to Captain and Mrs. Bench."

A sympathetic KGB agent smuggled a copy of the Denver newspaper into Doctor Khrushova's clinic. After reading it, she looked up, clasped her hands under her chin, and a broad smile crossed over her face.

About the Author

USAF photo. Final mission over Vietnam.

COLONEL ROBERT MCCARTAN SERVED twenty-eight years in the U.S. Air Force. He amassed more than 5,000 flying hours, including 3,000 in the B-47 bomber. He flew 156 combat missions in Vietnam in the EB-66 aircraft, most of them over North Vietnam. He taught four years at the Air Force Academy, served as an operations staff officer in the Pentagon, and commanded an Air Force wing. He earned a master's degree from the University of Denver. In 2004, McCartan published a memoir, *My Journey*. This is his first novel. Colonel McCartan resides in Arizona.

Printed in the United States
200588BV00003B/121-159/A

9 781587 369216